I0531667

Stories from Stourton: The Black Cat Gallery

by

Susan Hibberd

Susan Hibberd studied at the Dorset Institute of Higher Education before being awarded a BA at Southampton University. After almost a decade as an Internal Auditor in the Civil Service, she gave up full-time work, and now works part-time as a school librarian, which allows her to devote time to her creative interests. She lives in Kent where she is well known for her papermaking and community art work.

This book is sold subject to the condition that it shall not, by way of trade or otherwise, be lent, resold, hired out, or otherwise circulated without the publisher's prior consent in any form of binding or cover other than that in which it is published and without a similar condition including this condition being imposed on the subsequent publisher.

The moral right of Susan Hibberd has been asserted.

©Susan Hibberd 2017

Chapter One

'Oh, it's beautiful!' cooed Eleanor. She pushed hard against the heavy oak door, stepped over a pile of junk mail and led her friends into the empty building.

'You said that about the others as well,' Justin reminded her, sniffing as he looked around him. 'At least this one doesn't smell damp.'

He knew Lucy and William were ready to leave, having followed Eleanor around three empty premises already, each in a different village, but she seemed oblivious to their discomfort and treated them to a beaming smile as she trotted up to the first floor, knocking dust from the banister rail as she went.

William looked pointedly at Justin and tapped his watch. He jerked his head towards Lucy who stood watching the first spots of rain through the front window. She had her hands tucked under her arms and was shuffling her feet to keep them warm. If she got any colder he knew they'd *all* be having a really miserable afternoon. Justin rolled his eyes, sighed and went after Eleanor.

'That pub down the road looked OK,' William called up the stairs. He could hear Eleanor enthusing about the layout of the living accommodation while Justin was trying to hurry her along. 'We'll meet you in there, shall we?'

Without waiting for an answer, he dug in his pocket for the car keys and jingled them at Lucy. 'Come on, we'll get the drinks in.' He grinned as he pointed his key fob through the window gunslinger-style and made a shooting noise. Somehow he never got over his boyish delight at making the lights flash by remote control.

Lucy followed him out to the car without speaking. In fact, now that he thought about it, she hadn't spoken for quite a while.

'Well, what do you think?' he asked. Lucy slammed the car door and thrust the seat belt home.

'I *think* it's freezing cold, and I *think* I want to go home,' she said, leaning forward to turn up the heating. 'I

2

agreed to come here for a nice lazy weekend in a cosy hotel. I didn't expect to be dragged around the middle of nowhere looking at stupid little shops.' She tucked her hands under her arms again and leant back in the seat. Despite her expensively-coloured blonde hair, pulled back in a deceptively simple style and her carefully applied make-up, there was something in her look which was not altogether attractive.

William had to concentrate as he drove along the narrow lanes. The light rain was just enough to make visibility poor, but not quite enough to warrant the use of the wipers. It was only three o'clock, but the low clouds made it seem later. He was used to well-lit roads with ample space to overtake, not these winding B-roads that were crumbling away at the sides. Mud washed across the carriageway and every time a vehicle came in the opposite direction he had to squash his Alpha into the hedge to let it pass. Anyone else would have waited when at the nearest passing place, but not William.

He glanced at Lucy, huddled into the new Berber jacket she had bought especially for this trip, still scowling, and he had to admit that the weekend had been completely different from the one they had planned. He couldn't wait to get to the pub for a quick drink before going back to the hotel for a decent dinner so he could forget this miserable weather. The countryside in May was not something he'd be visiting again any time soon.

Back at the vacant property, Justin had given up trying to convince Eleanor that she had seen enough and that it was time for afternoon tea. He had retreated to the car, where the warmth of the heater and a CD of Haydn were doing a lot to calm him down. He tipped the seat back and closed his eyes for a minute, letting the music wash over him. He loved this car, and was more than happy to spend time in it. He glanced back at the empty property, and as Eleanor was still nowhere to be seen, he adjusted the heating and leant back in his seat.

Eleanor, meanwhile, had pulled a sketchbook from her bag and was noting down design ideas in broad strokes of

3

colour. The building had been one of three pubs in Stourton, and although it had long since been converted into a private home, it still retained many of the original features. She loved the fact that the long mahogany bar still stood in the main sitting room, and that there was a large cellar. Just thinking about the dark, unexplored depths gave her a thrill of excitement.

Each of the successive owners had put their own stamp on the property, but each had done their best to keep the character of the building intact. Estate Agents would describe it as being 'solidly built', and the wood panelling and deep window recesses gave the place an air of permanence. It had been built to offer a touch of luxury to weary travellers, and although the back rooms were less well-finished, the public rooms had all been created from local materials by local craftsmen.

Perched on the edge of what was once the bar, Eleanor leant against a column, put her head on one side and stopped to consider for a moment. She knew her hair was full of dust and cobwebs and that her black jeans were now a shade of grey that could only be described as 'dishwater'. She realised that her hands and nails were dirtier than they had been in years where she had been opening windows and running her fingers along architraves and dado rails. And she was painfully aware that her friends were waiting for her and were going to be very annoyed when she finally turned up.

But somehow she was finding it hard to tear herself away from this place. Was it the quietness, broken only by the song of the birds? Was it the way she was able to move from room to room without ever losing her sense of direction? Or was it the almost palpable pulsing of the history of the place that made her feel so at home?

She tucked her hair behind her ears and thought for a moment before jumping down. She quickly ran round each room, taking a few photos in each.

She knew Justin was waiting for her, and although she would like to have spent more time in the property, she also wanted to please him.

Justin was just the kind of boyfriend her mother would want for her. Handsome, cheeky, devil-may-care, with a good pedigree and an excellent job. Apart from the odd argument, they got on well enough, although Eleanor sometimes suspected he might be rather shallow. Oh well, time would tell, she thought, slamming the front door behind her and skipping over to the car.

'Okey-doke,' she said brightly as she got in and pecked Justin on the cheek, 'All finished. Thanks for waiting.'

Justin smiled weakly, started the car, and turned towards the town. He was usually proud of the fact that Eleanor was different from the rest of their crowd, but today there was something else about her. Something he didn't recognise; something that worried him. He began to chat about a play they'd listened to on the radio while driving down, but Eleanor was flicking through the photos on her phone and hardly heard a word.

After drinks at the pub the friends dropped off the keys at the estate agents and ventured out for a short walk in the countryside. However, the combination of constant drizzle, overgrown pathways and Lucy's non-stop commentary about the shortcomings of the area soon drove them back indoors.

They had started out well enough, taking the tow-path along the side of the river, but when they had turned to come back they had chosen a different path. This one soon became overgrown, and Lucy complained that her trousers were getting soaked as she pushed past the dripping fronds of the hedgerow plants.

'Where does it all come from?' she asked, rhetorically, 'Is there anywhere we can go that doesn't have green stuff everywhere?'

Even more of a problem was the clouds of insects that flew up from the bushes as they passed. Lucy and William were convinced that they were mosquitoes, and despite

5

Eleanor's assurance that it was the wrong time of year they were frightened that they were going to get bitten. Lucy's constant shrieking soon began to grate on Eleanor's nerves and as they path became even narrower it became evident that they would need to turn back.

By the time they got back to the hotel they were damp from top to toe and they all opted for a hot shower before meeting again in the hotel bar.

They ordered afternoon tea, which they ate in the hotel bar, and then returned to their hotel rooms. They piled onto the beds, fluffed up the pillows and filled in the time before dinner by streaming a film on the large-screen TV.

To their surprise, the hotel provided an excellent dinner and even boasted a cellar that lived up to William's unreasonably high expectations. The service was impeccable and the sounds of a folk band from the public bar sounded rustic and merry, not coarse and comical as the Maître d' had worried. He had pointed them out to the waitress when they first arrived, and warned her to be careful. He knew their type, he said, and they could be very demanding.

They were now sipping coffee, nibbling on mint chocolates and wondering whether to have brandy at the table or in one of the comfortable double rooms they had booked.

'Well,' said Lucy, flicking her bleached blonde hair out of her eyes. 'I vote we go upstairs, snuggle under the duvet and watch a film. That way we can try to forget where we are until the morning.' She looked ruefully at her glass. 'What a shame we ordered all that wine, or we could have driven back this evening.'

Eleanor looked up from her phone in surprise. 'Do you really hate it that much?' she asked.

Her friend took the phone from her hand, glanced at it and saw the photos. 'You know I love you, Eleanor, but you've hardly said one word to us all evening. You've been flicking through these photos like you were re-reading texts from a new boyfriend.'

She passed the phone back to Eleanor. 'Put it away, for goodness sake, and let's have some fun. Look – how much do you bet I can get that boy at the bar to ask me out?' She tottered unsteadily towards the bar, pretending to be drunk, and draped an arm around the neck of a boy who couldn't have been more than nineteen. Her cut-glass accent, plunging neckline and killer heels seemed out-of-place in the cosy bar, and were obviously a surprise to the young man she was teasing. On any other day, Eleanor would have joined Justin and William in their lewd remarks, but today she felt differently. She pushed back her chair and nodded to the waitress.

'Can you put that on our bill, please? Justin, I'll see you upstairs.'

Climbing the stairs alone, Eleanor tried to put her finger on what it was that was worrying her. She was in a lovely hotel with her very best friends in the world, and had just eaten a marvellous meal. But something niggled at her. She couldn't get the old pub out of her mind.

Sitting in the window-seat of the hotel room, looking out over the moonlit grounds, she listened to the soaring violins and merry banjos of the band. She heard the sound of the audience clapping as one song finished and another began. The light from the hotel spilled out into the night and lit up the small herb garden. The fields beyond were smudged with silver from the moon and rippled with the wildlife within. Looking out onto the scene with her city eyes, it seemed to Eleanor that the line between the two wavered with each breath of the night.

What was it like, she wondered, to have lived in the same village all your life? To have grown up with the same houses, the same trees and the same people around you? To know almost everyone who lived with a ten mile radius?

Eleanor herself had grown up in a bustling city, looked after by a string of foreign nannies, hardly seeing her parents from one day to the next. At eighteen she had left home to go to university and had never found her way back home. Changing jobs and locations every two or three years had left her with no roots, a huge number of friends that she only spoke to on Facebook and a feeling that she was missing out on life.

Her parents had recently bought a house in Scotland, so she now saw them even more rarely than before. When they went abroad, they would fly from Glasgow, so their trips to London were few and far between.

On impulse, she grabbed a jumper, ran downstairs and slipped out of the French windows into the patio garden. Standing in the cold night air, she shivered and thrust her hands into her pockets for warmth. The Victorian planters and moss-covered paving stones of the walled garden gave the space an air of timeless antiquity, thrown into sharp relief by the noisy revelry behind her. The light from the doorway darkened the shadows and intensified into highlights which shimmered as the curtains blew in the breeze.

She felt she was standing on the edge of time. The chill of the garden contrasting with the warmth that seemed to come from the hotel. She started to imagine the people who might have stood where she was now standing, their dresses sweeping the floor and their cloaks pulled tightly up to their necks against the cold night air.

Just as she started to become lost in the day-dream, the patio door burst open and a couple ran into the garden, bringing with them a wave of warm air and music. They stood for a moment, nonplussed by finding someone in front of them.

'Oh, sorry,' the boy began, 'I didn't realise anyone was out here...' The girl giggled nervously, and started to pull her lover back indoors.

Eleanor shook her head, waving away the apology. 'Not a problem,' she replied, 'I was just going to go inside anyway.'

Having been brought right back to the present day with such speed, Eleanor decided to turn in for the night. She found her way back to her room, passing the restaurant on the way. Her friends were still in in the bar, and seemed to be ordering more drinks. She could tell that they were settling in for the evening, as they took up more chairs than they needed. By the end of the evening they would have covered twice the amount of space they merited and be louder than everyone else in the bar put together. It was odd to be looking at them from the outside, and far from being proud that she was usually one of this group, she was beginning to feel a bit ashamed at some of her previous behaviour.

Leaving the curtains open so she could see the moon and the stars, Eleanor snuggled down in the bed and reached for her phone.

She had photographs from each of the properties they had visited that day, interspersed with ones of Justin, William and Lucy, but it was the ones from the old pub that drew her back.

Flicking through the last few, she was once again struck by the beauty of the place. It seemed to be caught in a loop of time, unable to restart without the right catalyst.

What was it that the building was waiting for? What was it that made it seem so right for her?

She started to think about how she might furnish and decorate the place if it was hers. Looking at the large living area which had once been the main bar, she saw it as a long gallery, showing off her collection of artworks and without a conscious connection, she started to think that the small snug would make a fabulous studio area.

She caught herself mid-thought and almost laughed out loud. She had never painted anything in her life, and this certainly wasn't the time in her life when she should be thinking about taking up a hobby. She was still in the middle of building her career!

Flicking quickly to the end of the sequence, she was ready to put the phone down when something in the corner of one of the photographs caught her eye. She could make out the outline of a black cat sitting on one of the windowsills. She couldn't image how she had missed it when she had been in the room. Zooming in, she saw that it was a surprisingly large cat, and that the marking on its face gave it a look of constant enquiry. How funny!

'It's obviously his home,' she thought to herself, unconsciously stroking the picture with one finger. 'It's The Black Cat Pub.'

She switched off the light and pulled the duvet up over her nose. 'Or The Black Cat Gallery.'

Chapter Two

The next day, Eleanor woke up early and decided not to wake the others. She dressed quickly and creeping past William and Lucy's room and wandered down to the restaurant. She ordered a light breakfast and sat listening to the chatter of the other early risers and looking out of the window. After the rain of the previous day, Sunday had dawned bright and sunny. The waitress leant over and opened the top windows to let in some air, and Eleanor could smell the freshness of the newly-washed foliage. Above the quiet murmur of voices, she could hear the birdsong. It all seemed so idyllic.

Some of the other guests told the waitress they were planning a day of short walks around the area and asked her if she had any recommendations. Listening to the reply, Eleanor realised that she knew nothing about where she currently lived in London. If anyone asked her about walks around her apartment, she would have no idea. She used the light railway or tube for short journeys and her car for longer journeys, hardly walking anywhere. She was a member of the local gym, and that was where she took her exercise.

When the others came down, she could see that they were rather the worse for wear. Lucy had dressed with her normal care, in skin-tight jeans teamed with a hand-knitted cardigan and looked immaculate as usual, but there were dark circles under her eyes and her face had lost its normal animation. Always looking for excitement, the bar of The Kings Head had obviously provided it for her last night. She looked as if she was now ready to sleep for the rest of the weekend.

'Where did you get to?' Lucy asked. 'We had a fabulous night,' she looked around her, as if trying to remember where she was, 'not that I can remember all of it!' She laughed, and Eleanor was astounded to find herself thinking that her friend was shallow, when previously she had thought of her ditsy nature as being cute and fun, with part of her wanting to be more like Lucy and less like Eleanor.

Justin's curt 'good morning' was rather cool, and Eleanor realised that she might have put his nose out of joint by deserting them the night before. Oh well, it couldn't be helped now, and she tried to make it up to him by suggesting that they went to a recital together in the week.

'What do you want to do today?' Eleanor asked, as the boys ploughed through their full English breakfasts and Lucy picked at her toast and sniffed at the orange juice.

'If you're asking me, I'd like to get back in time to have dinner at The Riverside.'

Eleanor looked at her to see if she was serious.

'So you don't want to see any more of Kent?' she asked.

Lucy gave her a hard stare, 'I've seen enough of Kent to last me a lifetime. I just can't understand why people would want to live all the way out here. It's so far from everywhere!'

'I don't mind driving around for a bit,' Justin offered, 'Is there anywhere we can drive to?'

There were no more properties to view, and Lucy put her foot down at the idea of revisiting any of the ones they had already seen, so in the end they paid their bill and decided to go straight back to London.

After an uneventful drive home, Eleanor slipped back into her old life. She worked as a personal shopper at one of the largest department stores in London and loved her job. However, she always wondered whether there was more to life than pushing a certain lifestyle onto people who had no idea of their own personal style. She sometimes wondered if they would be better off left to flounder and eventually find their own way, like a toddler learning to walk. There would be a few mishaps, but how else were they to learn?

Eleanor certainly had style. Her style was the flamboyant mix of beautiful tailoring and printed cotton that the magazines called boho-chic, and she was the envy of the girls in her office.

Having grown up outside the city, she had a different attitude to life from her colleagues and wasn't afraid to speak her mind. These two things together kept her slightly apart from the rest of the office crowd, with some of them feeling jealous of her style and poise, and some feeling that she was judgemental and aloof.

The hair that fell to her shoulders was a rich brown, shading to almost black in places. She kept it cut in a razor-sharp bob that always looked immaculate, swinging as she walked but falling back into place when she stopped. Shunning the current craze for fake tan, her pale face stood out against its mahogany halo and her dark eyes shone under perfectly-formed eyebrows.

An outsider might think that Eleanor was one of a kind with the other girls, but people who took the time to get to know her well saw a different side. Although she worked in PR, Eleanor had a deep dislike of dissembling and avoided the people she considered to be shallow. Her creative side showed in her choice of dress and in the way she had designed the interior of her living space, but was as yet undeveloped. One day, she told herself, she would have time to paint, draw, throw pots or design clothing. For the moment, she needed to concentrate on her career, and her commitment and obvious skills were moving her up the corporate ladder at a very pleasing rate.

When she went back to work on the Monday she managed to avoid everyone's questions about the weekend and carried on her life as normal. In the daytime she rushed from interview to interview, typing madly on her PC in between times.

At lunchtime, her friend Elspeth spoke to her.

'A group of use are going to try out that new wine bar for lunch. Do you want to come?'

'No, thanks, I think I'll just eat at my desk today.'

'Oh come on,' her friend insisted, ' You can tell us all about the horrors of the countryside and remind us how great it is to live in London.'

Eleanor was amazed that her friend was so narrow-minded.

'Ah, but I might have liked it,' she countered, raising an eyebrow.

'Don't be silly, you're just the same as us. What could you possibly have found to like out in the middle of nowhere? Now you've got it out of your system you can forget about it. Come and try this new place with us and we can talk about Emily's hen party.'

Eleanor declined, and as predicted ate at her desk alone. She picked at her sandwich and spent some time wondering if she was making a complete fool of herself by thinking about changing her lifestyle and going to live in Kent. Perhaps she should just carry on with her life as it was.

In the evenings she watched TV, cleaned the house, and worked on the homework for her Art History class. Justin was away again on one of his frequent business trips, this time to the USA, although he usually only travelled as far as Europe. She'd be lucky if her phoned her once all the time he was away.

The one thing that did change in her life was the fact that every night before she went to bed she checked her phone. Not to see if Justin had called, as previously, but to look at the photos of the properties they had visited that weekend.

Again and again she returned to the ones of the old pub, planning what she might do with it if it were hers. She even drew out a floor plan of the place, using the estate agents' details to get the dimensions right.

By the end of two weeks, she had collected a lever-arch file full of papers and added a long list of Favourites to her web browser. What she had thought of as a passing fancy was turning out to be more like an obsession.

Sadly, one phone call to the estate agent was enough to put a huge damper on her enthusiasm.

'Oh, Ms Stratton,' purred the estate agent, putting undue emphasis on the 'Ms', 'I'm afraid I've got some bad news for you. The seller, Katherine Wilkinson rang this morning from Australia, where she now lives. She has now decided not to sell, but to rent out the property.'

'Can you tell me why that is? I thought she was keen to sell it.'

'Yes, I spoke with her only this morning. She's now decided to demolish the property and build houses on the site. She just needs to get planning permission and the right financial backing. I think she already has part of the finance in place, and now she wants to push ahead with the project.'

'What a shame. Do you know how long she wants to rent it for?'

'I think her timescale is twelve months,' she paused to gauge Eleanor's reaction, 'I can confirm that for you if you're interested.'

'Um, yes, please. If you wouldn't mind,' Eleanor's mind was racing, 'Actually, no, it doesn't matter. I'm not looking for a rental property. Thanks anyway.'

However, an hour later Eleanor was back on the phone, asking if she could pop down at the weekend to view the property again. With no clear idea in her mind of what she was going to do when she got there, she bundled an overnight bag into the car as she left home in the morning and straight after work on Friday she joined the queues on the M25.

As she drove, she noticed that the weather in Kent was completely different from the weather she had experienced previously, and the effect on the countryside was spectacular. Spring had finally arrived and many of the trees that lined the roads were in blossom, from the lacy fronds of the elderflower to the frosted icing of one or two self-seeded pears. Late afternoon sun slanted across the fields, making the driving difficult in some places, but shining with unbelievable beauty through the acid green of the new leaf growth in others. The smaller roads seemed even narrower as the verges reached inwards, and the branches of the hedgerow trees met over her head, creating a series of green tunnels, snaking through the fields.

Arriving in Stourton she went straight to the gallery, as she already called it, and pulled into the driveway. She knew that the property was empty, and had no qualms about disturbing any current tenants. The gravel was spotted with tufts of grass, the bushes were ragged and the yellowing paint on the front door was peeling, but the sight of the property made Eleanor smile. It felt to her as if she was coming home.

She was about to move the car to park it more neatly when a knock on the passenger-door window made her jump. She wound down the window and leant across to see who it was and she immediately regretted doing so. She should have opened her door and got out of the car to speak to the man who was scowling at her through the open window. Her first instinct was to pull her short skirt down over her knees. Fabulous as it looked in the office, it had not been designed for the modest driver.

Bending down to rest his arms on the car windowsill, with his hands hanging inside the car, it was difficult to estimate the man's height and she was instantly irritated by the intrusion into her thoughts and into her private space.

Her 'Yes?' came out more sharply than she intended, but he didn't move.

'You know you're trespassing by parking here, don't you?' he asked, his steady gaze taking in the untidiness of the car's interior and her navy business suit in one lazy sweep. He obviously thought she was another city banker looking for a second home. She shivered as his gaze swept up her exposed thighs, and past her expensive jewellery to the slightly discomfited look on her face. His eyes locked on hers and set against his calm stillness, the depths of his pupils seemed to be like black holes drawing her out and pulling her in. She wished that she had taken the time to change out of her work clothes before leaving London.

'Actually, the estate agent representing the owners said that it would be all right,' she said, hearing the lameness of the retort as she said it. 'Are you the owner?'

He nodded his understanding of her reason for being there and continued, 'Nick Preston. I might be seeing you around.' Before she could answer, he had straightened up and was walking away from the car.

She was slightly surprised that he didn't return to the road, but chose a Public Footpath that cut across the open fields. As he walked away, she could see that he was perhaps six feet tall, and had the upright, self-confident stride of a countryman used to walking miles. His clothes were good quality, but scuffed and rather dirty, as if he worked with his hands. He reminded her of a gentleman farmer, so secure in his heritage that he could be careless of his appearance.

Her fingers had itched to smooth back the lock of dirty blonde hair that had fallen into his eyes as he had leant forwards, so that she could see the colour of his eyes but she pushed that thought from her mind. In the dim interior of the car they had looked as if they were the dark brown of a winter chestnut. She hoped that she would have a chance to look more closely in the not-too-distant future.

'Get a grip,' she muttered to herself as she pulled the car closer to the house and put it into PARK.

As she walked around the house peering into the windows, she almost fell over the black cat who was sitting in an overgrown flower bed catching the last rays of the evening sun. The bricks had soaked up warmth during the day and now made the back wall to a cosy little den for the animal. He raised his head as she approached, as if wondering who had come to disturb his peaceful afternoon nap.

'Hello, Cat,' she said. She bent down to stroke him. 'Did you know you're in my photograph?' The cat looked as if it probably did.

'That stubble was only there because he hadn't bothered to shave,' she told it, unable to forget Nick Preston and his errant lock of hair. 'It wasn't a fashion statement.' The cat seemed to agree, because it rubbed itself against her knees and looked at the door as if asking to be let in.

'Oh, I'm sorry,' she said, 'I don't have a key. I'll come back tomorrow and we can look round together.' She stroked him until he grew bored and wandered off to another part of the garden.

After walking around the outside for a while, and looking through a few more windows, Eleanor realised that the day had grown a lot colder. The stones of the patio garden had warmed during the day, but there was a chill in the air. Saying goodbye to the cat, who had finished his circuit of the garden and come back inside, she retraced her steps to the car and drove to the hotel they had used before to have a hot bath and to think seriously about her future.

Chapter Three

The next day she got up early, ate breakfast in her room and drove into Stourton to get the key from the estate agent.

She was annoyed to find that they had already given the key to another prospective tenant, but agreed to go back in an hour's time to see if it had been returned .

Parking her car, she walked onto the main street and looked left and right. In both directions she could see the picture-perfect chocolate-box image of an English country village, punctuated by a surprisingly small number of advertising signs from multinational companies. The local town council obviously cared deeply about preserving the town's historical look. She stopped to take a few photographs as she walked, and noticed that this marked her out as an outsider. She worried about this for a minute and then decided to be proud of her status as 'tourist'; after all, tourism was one of the main ways the townspeople made their money.

The largely medieval houses were interspersed with some lovely Victorian and Edwardian buildings, many of which were still shops, as originally intended. Stourton still had its own butcher, baker and greengrocer, as well as several other independents. Many of them had old-fashioned awnings, which jutted out over the pavements, casting pools of shade for the customer. Cars lined the narrow streets, and the pavements were beginning to fill up, even at this early hour.

Used as she was to the throng of London, Eleanor was happy to find that she could walk along very easily, stopping to look into shop windows as she went. All about her she heard the buzz that is associated with a small town. By no means did everyone know everyone else, but there were a significant number of 'Hello's, 'Good Morning's and 'How are you today's. This was in stark contrast to a walk down a

London street, when the chances of meeting anyone you knew were slim.

She stopped in front of a shop that was either a very old interior design shop or a very up-to-date vintage retail outlet. She stopped to decide which. The premises seemed to be literally bursting with merchandise, which was spilling out of the door and onto the street outside.

As she watched, the shop's owner started to pull a large rattan bookshelf through the doorway, catching it on the doors hinges as she did so. She gave it an irritable tug, cursing mildly as she did so.

'Here, let me help,' said Eleanor, taking one end of the unit and guiding it through the doorway.

'Oh, thanks,' replied the owner, pushing her hair out of her eyes. 'I'm running a bit late this morning. As usual!' She put down the bookshelf, pushed at her hair again and quickly started to arrange antique books and hand-embroidered linens on the shelf. She hummed a country-and-western song as she worked, and Eleanor thought how idyllic it was to be laying out your shop in the sunshine in a beautiful village like Stourton, happy in the knowledge that the day would most likely be a good one.

She stood back for a moment, and then said 'Are those tablecloths hand-embroidered? They might look nice on the mangle at the back. It would look as if they had just been washed. And then you could bring those paperweights forward and put them next to the books.' The shop owner stopped what she was doing and stood up.

Turning red, Eleanor started to apologise, as she realised that she might have been giving unwanted advice. She needn't have worried.

'Now why didn't I see that myself?' asked the lady, re-arranging the items. 'You'd better come inside and see what else you can help me with.'

Eleanor laughed. The lady's abruptness seemed somehow down-to-earth and comforting, not as rude as it seemed at face value. She came across as someone you could trust, and Eleanor was herself a fan of speaking her mind. As she had been going to look round the shop anyway, Eleanor ducked inside, following the flash of red hair and dirndl skirting.

Inside, she found an Aladdin's cave of retro chic. The walls were lined with distressed shelving painted in various shades of chalky white and they were filled with pottery and ceramics from all eras. King Charles Spaniels sat next to hand-painted Art Deco cups and saucers and tall Wedgewood vases towered over hand-built Troika-inspired mugs from the 1970s. The mix was unexpected, quirky and yet totally enthralling.

At the very back of the shop was a Welsh dresser full of stoneware glazed in a palette of blues and greens. It made one think instantly of the sea on a warm summer's day, drenched in the hottest of suns.

Ignoring the more traditional pieces, Eleanor went straight to a large open platter that had been glazed in cobalt blue and splashed with copper.

'Wow,' she said, sliding her hands underneath to pick it up and feeling the texture of the glaze with her thumbs. 'This is great.' Placing one hand in the middle, she flipped it over to see the maker's mark and was disappointed not to find one. 'Who made these?' she asked.

'Oh, they're just some of the things I knock out,' came a voice from behind the counter accompanied by a jangling of coins as the day's float was poured into a container. 'Rosie McAlister at your service.'

Eleanor put down the platter and held out her hand. 'Eleanor Stratton,' she said as they shook hands warmly.

'So what do you think?' asked Rosie, pushing at her hair with one hand and waving the other around the shop. Eleanor wondered how someone so seemingly disorganised could run such a beautifully-displayed shop. Rosie was dressed like the archetypal rural potter in a long loose-fitting dress and a hand-knitted cardigan. She reached under the counter for a length of cotton fabric, used it to tie back her hair. She pushed once more at some errant strands and sat down.

'It's all right, isn't it?'

'All right?' echoed Eleanor. 'It's *lovely*!'

Looking around the shop again, she started to enthuse about the space. 'It's full but not too cluttered, bright but not too in-you-face, it's full of interesting objects,' she stopped to pick up an 1950s Homemaker plate 'of all ages. And you've managed to fit your own work in with the vintage stuff very cleverly. I think it's perfect.'

She moved a pile of pre-war annuals from an Edwardian nursing chair and sat down. 'I could move in and live here quite happily,' she grinned, leaning forward to pick up a one-eyed teddy bear.

Rosie laughed with her and waved a mug in her direction. 'Peppermint tea?'

'We only drink tea from mugs that have been handmade by local potters,' said Eleanor mock-seriously, looking at the bear for confirmation.

'Then you're in luck.'

In between serving a string of customers, many of whom seemed to come in for a chat rather than to buy anything, Rosie told Eleanor a bit about Stourton.

Due to its location and its beautiful mixture of architectural buildings, the town had been able to retain its place as the main market town of the area. One of the churches had been deconsecrated and turned into a Village Hall, and more people shopped in the out-of-town retail centre than in the local shops, but essentially it was very much as it had been for hundreds of years.

Eleanor wondered whether to ask her about Nick Preston, but decided against it. She was yet to clarify her feelings about him, and in the meantime she kept the memory of their short encounter tucked away inside her like an unwrapped present. Instead she asked Rosie about the old pub.

'Oh, The Hall Arms you mean?' asked Rosie. 'The previous tenants didn't look after it very well and it's been on the market for ages. I doubt they'll get a buyer for it in that state.'

'I don't think they want a buyer,' said Eleanor, ' The owner's trying to get planning permission to build houses on the site.' Rosie looked sad.

'Really? It's such a shame that so many old buildings are being pulled down. They are part of our heritage – as a country, not just locally – and really should be kept in good repair.'

A small woman wearing a cream cardigan covered with embroidered purple flowers came into the shop and Rosie jumped up. 'I'll have to tell you about that another time. Jan's going to look after the shop for a bit while I pop out. Come back and see me after you've had another look at the pub.'

'Oh. That's fine. I'll just....Umm...' Eleanor struggled for words while she fumbled for her bag, but by the time she had found it Rosie had rushed out of the door and left her friend in charge, so she finished with 'Well, it was nice meeting you. Goodbye then...' and walked outside into the sunshine.

Picking up a take-away coffee and a Danish pastry from the shop next door to the estate agents, Eleanor drove back to The Hall Arms. It was sad that it was going to be knocked down, she knew, and she wished that she was the kind of person who could take it on, breathe new life into it and become a well-known local figure like Rosie McAlister obviously was. She fantasised briefly about being a local celebrity, being invited to tea with the Mayor and opening to Church fete. Oh well, it wasn't going to happen, but at least she'd had a nice weekend down here, pottering around.

The sun was shining into her face as she came up to the building, dazzling her, so she walked around to the back, where she found a little courtyard garden. Shielded from the breeze, she sat on a low wall and ate her pastry, sharing the last crumbs with the cat that had appeared as soon as she had arrived.

The neglected garden looked as if no-one had tended it for months, and plants were pushing their way up through the paving slabs. She brushed her hands over the new growth of a lemon balm plant and breathed in the sharp citrus smell that was released. Overhead, heavy boughs of hawthorn were loaded with May blossom, the petals dropping onto the flagstones like forgotten confetti. As she looked around, she felt a sense of complete calm as if she had been running around and only now been able to stop for a rest. She breathed deeply and felt the stillness permeate her soul.

Roused from her reverie by the harsh cries of some squabbling starlings, she finished her drink, unlocked the back door and walked into the house. As she did so, she felt something brush past her legs and moved aside as the cat sped in through the cat flap before she could open the door.

'So that's how you managed to get into my photo!' she laughed. 'Well, you're a sneaky one, aren't you?' She bent down to pet him for a while.

'But I don't live here yet, so I can't feed you. Sorry.'

The house felt cold after the warmth of the sunshine in the garden and Eleanor shivered as she went into the lounge. It took her eyes a few minutes to adjust to the darkness, as the curtains had been left closed. Motes of dust shimmered in the shafts of light that pierced the darkness like one of the best atmospheric photographs and shadows breathed into the corners. Once again, she had the feeling that something was about to happen. It was as if she was watching a film of her own life and was waiting for the climax.

Shaking off the feeling, she walked from room to room, seriously planning what she might do with each one. She had come on the first visit as a bit of a joke, just to see what might be possible. Now she began to feel that what had at first been a dream might become a reality.

The master bedroom had a built-in window seat overlooking the North Downs, and gave a fantastic view over the rolling hills and patchwork of fields. She could see sheep in one of the fields, and wondered if the white blobs she could just make out were lambs. She promised herself she would walk down and have look later on, if she had time. The fields were outlined with bands of dark green, and she thought about all the wildlife that must live there, right on the doorstep of this wonderful old house.

Eleanor was glad that she had brought her laptop with her rather than leaving it at the hotel. She pulled out the details of the property and looked through them once more, spreading the papers around her where she sat.

Using her phone, she checked her online bank account, and opened an Excel spreadsheet to work out the costs that might be involved in the project.

The cat curled up in a pool of sunlight in the centre of the room, stretching before he settled down to sleep, and Eleanor treated him to a running commentary of her thoughts:

'I'd need to give a month's notice at work, you know. I can't just leave,' she told him. 'But that would give me a month's wages in hand. Add to that the ISA savings, plus the savings in *this* account and I get the figure at the bottom here. Are you taking any notice of me?'

The cat sniffed in her direction, which she took to be an acknowledgement of his understanding. She leant forward and brushed away a ball of dust that had caught on his whiskers.

'Anyway, I can probably rent out the flat.' She looked at the cat for approval. 'It *is* in a very desirable London location,' she reminded him. 'So, if I take into account my living expenses and the rent for this place, add *this*, and take away *that*, we get a total monthly excess of....gosh!'

Chapter Four

Eight weeks later, Eleanor's life had changed dramatically. She had made the radical decision to move away from London and take a chance on the gallery, leaving her London life behind her and hoping that she might find a direction to her life by moving out of the fast lane and into the country.

The HR Department had convinced her to take a one-year sabbatical rather than handing in her notice altogether, her friend Elspeth was keen to rent her London flat, and she had found that there was really very little that she wanted to take down to Kent with her. Somewhat disconcertingly, this included Justin.

Of course, there was a terrific row when Eleanor told Justin that she was going to give up work to live in Kent for a year. She wined and dined him at her flat before dropping the bombshell, but it still hit him hard.

'You can't just leave us all and go to live in some God-forsaken corner of the countryside where you don't even know anyone,' he shouted, standing up and storming into the kitchen to tower over her.

Eleanor remained calm. 'Oh, I think I can,' was all she said as she continued to sort out her cupboards. 'In fact, I've already signed the papers.' She dumped some almost-empty cereal packets in the bin, pleased at the symbolism of the act.

'What?' Justin stuttered, 'When?' Although she was annoyed at his obvious belief that she should have consulted him first, Eleanor was vaguely flattered at his reaction. At least he cared that she was leaving.

'The weekend you flew to Germany, I went to Kent. I met the letting agent and we signed the papers there and then. I now hold the lease for the next twelve months. Elspeth is moving in here on the fifteenth and I shall be moving to the gallery.'

'"Gallery"' scoffed Justin, 'Are you even listening to yourself? It's just an old pub.' He paced up and down the room, looking down at the traffic on The Thames, which ran

26

past her loft-apartment window. This particular flat had been the show home when the block was developed and had every conceivable benefit. Justin had always thought that one day he might end up living in the apartment as one half of a happy couple. He stopped pacing and rested his hands on the windowsill, locking his elbows and resting his head against the glass. Eleanor waited for him to move on to his next point.

'Anyway, what makes you think people want to drive out into the middle of nowhere just to buy a picture? We've got more than enough galleries here in town. All nicely accessible.'

He stomped around for a while more, and then picked up his car keys. 'I'll see you later, then,' he said. She turned her head as he leant in for his customary kiss, so he caught her cheek instead of her mouth and as the door closed behind him and the words 'or perhaps not' sprung into her mind. This was going to be a huge change to her life.

Once the door had closed behind him, it struck Eleanor what it was about the man that irritated her. He always needed to be in control. Almost every time she suggested that they watch a film or go to a play, he had a better suggestion. Every time she wanted to stay in he wanted to go out, and every time she wanted to go out, he wanted to stay in. She wondered why she hadn't noticed it before.

'Oh, well,' she thought, 'I'll phone him later and make up.'

***

Eleanor had taken out a one-year tenancy on the property and agreed that she would take it part-furnished. She booked a room at the hotel for her first week in Stourton, but when she collected the keys and walked into the house she found that she couldn't bear to leave it. She felt somehow as if this was her home already, and it seemed silly to go anywhere else, so she rang to cancel her booking. The girl who answered had a slight Kentish burr to her voice that Eleanor found refreshing after the clipped, affected accents of London.

'There's something about the place that gets under your skin, isn't there?' the receptionist had laughed. 'I'm sorry you're not staying with us, but I'm glad to have another free room. We get really busy in this run-up to the holidays and once the weather gets warmer, everyone wants to come before the kids get out of school. Don't forget that you don't have to be a guest to eat in the restaurant. Perhaps we'll see you down here one evening?'

'You're a great salesperson,' smiled Eleanor, 'and I might just do that.' She said goodbye, ended the call and slipped the mobile back into her handbag. Her first thought was that she would need to get the landline reconnected, but no sooner had she done so, than her mobile began to ring again. The Estate Agent was calling to let her know that the owner had forgotten to mention a prior arrangement. They had agreed with a local carpenter that he could take some seasoned wood from one of the outbuildings and they wanted her to know that he might come to collect it without knowing she was already in residence.

Eleanor assured the Estate Agent that this wouldn't be a problem and found her curiosity piqued by the mention of outhouses. She opened as many windows as she could to let in the light and blow out the cobwebs and wandered into the master bedroom again.

It was a fabulous room, with low ceilings, exposed beams and whitewashed walls. The wooden floors had been sanded and waxed and there was a fantastic cast iron fireplace still in place. To many, it might have seemed like a bit of a cliché, but it suited Eleanor's mood down to the ground. The windows were small, but had been replaced with double-glazed units. They sat deep within the thick walls, giving a wide window sill that could almost double as a seat. Perfect for a vase of seasonal flowers picked from the garden.

She leant out of the windows and took in the view. It was truly spectacular. Past the ragged profusion that was the unkempt garden of the property was an orchard. Rows of pear and apple trees stood like a waiting bridal party, decked out in their pink and white finery and she could hear small birds quarrelling in branches. The different shades of blossom showed that the farmer had planted several different fruit varieties and she wondered what they would be when they matured.

She could just see the roofs of the outhouses she was looking for, and caught a glimpse of some house martins flying up under the roofs of some of them. She wondered what they were doing and decided to take a closer look.

Passing through the courtyard garden she came out into a large coach yard surrounded by old stables. The gravel was patchy and several of the stables were boarded up, but she could imagine how it might have looked with coaches swinging in to change horses while their occupants, stiff from the journey bundled into the inn for refreshments.

Eleanor pulled on her jacket and walked across to the stable block, and looked into one or two. Several were so dilapidated that they were almost falling down already, but one or two looked as if they had only recently been vacated.

She tugged open the door of one and walked inside. Although dim, she could see the outlines of the beams and the stalls that still stood. It had been subjected to a rudimentary cleaning, but wisps of straw still stuck to every surface. She sniffed the smell of hay and horse with satisfaction. The thought even briefly crossed her mind that she might keep a horse herself. Her pony-riding days were long gone, however, and it was unlikely that she would ever have the time or spare cash to have horses while she was here.

She pulled out her phone and snapped a few photographs of discarded tools beautifully lit by the sunshine that squeezed through broken shutters, thinking that they might come in useful as publicity shots at some stage. She also managed to get one or two of the house martins, who were nesting underneath the eves. Making sure the doors were secure, she turned to look at the house.

The building was on a hill; an appropriate resting-place for horses that had been asked to pull a significant weight up what was quite a steep incline. The roofline of the house was irregular, as the building had been added to time and time again over the centuries. She could place some of the architectural details, and thought that it would be interesting to trace the history of the building. The Kent peg tiles on the roof had been carried over onto each successive extension, and created an integral cover over the whole. The exterior, although made of a variety of different materials, had all been painted the same light cream, and the building looked well-maintained on the outside, although she knew that there was a lot of work to do inside.

Shielding her eyes from the full glare of the sun, Eleanor turned and looked out over the countryside. The hill sloped down into a valley, and she could see the occasional glint of light on water where the River Stour travelled through it. The traditional patchwork pattern of fields was clearly visible and they were tagged by groups of farm buildings. Cars moved along the lanes and it wasn't until she thought about the relative size of the vehicles that she realised how far away they were. She knew that the view was even more spectacular from the upper windows, and she thought that she must come back to take some photos from up there as well.

To the left was a range of hills, shielding the motorway from view, and to the right were the outskirts of Stourton. Her village. Her home.

Eleanor felt a strong sense of satisfaction when she thought about what she had achieved so far and went back into the house. However, as she began to take stock of the work that needed to be completed, she started to wonder if she had, indeed, made the right decision.

She would need to speak to the local Planning Officer to see what changes would need to be made to make the building suitable for commercial use, such as adding disabled access. Luckily there were plenty of rooms, and she had no trouble finding enough space for her own needs as well as for the gallery. She would concentrate on getting them up to standard and complete other rooms as she needed them. She was, after all, only renting and would be wasting money if she made more changes than were strictly necessary.

She decided that she would live upstairs, as the original publicans would have done, and chose a bedroom for herself and a sitting room. That was all she needed for now. There would originally have been a small upstairs kitchen for family use, but the current trend for kitchen diners had encouraged the last owner to reinstate the large kitchen downstairs.

It was an impressive room, decorated in a country style, and would double as a perfect dining area once it had been cleaned and polished. Eleanor was worried to see a large Aga cooker in the corner, but was relieved when she spotted a gas hob and oven as well. The cupboards were clean and fitted around the irregular shape of the kitchen with just enough nooks and crannies left to make it interesting. Eleanor could already see where she would put a wine rack, a painting and her favourite ceramic bowl.

Downstairs, the large public lounge had been retained as a living room, and there was very little work to be done to make it into a gallery space. Most of the work involved stripping out the modern features and installing commercial lighting. A wire hanging system would be a must, and she would need a system of plinths or shelving to display 3D work.

Apart from the main gallery, Eleanor nominated two downstairs rooms for gallery use: an office and a store room. She had decided that it would be necessary to keep her home life and her work life as separate as possible and planned to decorate each space in a distinct style to highlight the difference. The conservatory off the living room would be used as a seating area, and she could serve refreshments there during Private View evenings.

Eleanor had no experience in house renovation, but her skills in organising other people would stand her in good stead. She had agreed with the owner via the letting agent that she could make minor changes to the building as long as she sought consent for any major changes. She agreed to this happily, as she had no intention of spending more money than she needed to on a property she was only renting for a year. The other reason this suited her, was that it was always her policy to be cautious and she never rushed into things if she could help it. This fact alone made it all the more surprising that she had chosen to move to Stourton. Perhaps some things were just meant to be.

Chapter Five

Over the coming four weeks, she interviewed workmen, and plotted schedules for them to come and make the changes she needed. Deciding which order the work needed to be carried out in was a bit of a headache to start with, but with the help of local builder Mike she soon got the hang of it. It all came down to common sense in the end, and she soon had a steady stream of workmen banging, drilling, painting and carpeting in what was to be the gallery space.

While the work carried on in the house, Eleanor took the opportunity to explore the local area. She visited the local major towns and also spent some time travelling round the smaller villages tracking down some of the smaller antique shops. She came home with lots of bargains and also a few more extravagant treats. She was getting to know the area better and found out that although a few artists lived her and joined the local Open Studio scheme each year, there was no local gallery. This either meant that there was a gap in the market or that there was no call for one. Time would tell.

Each day, she took some time to speak to Mike and she found that they got on well together. He was only ten or fifteen years older than she was, but always seemed to be on hand at the right time with some acute saying or sound advice. She began to regard him as a father figure and looked forward to their frequent chats. They often sat in the garden and shared a pot of tea and a packet of Bourbon biscuits as he went over how work on the gallery was progressing. Once the business was over, they chatted about friends and family, and found that they shared the same wicked sense of humour. Eleanor could always rely on Mike to see the same funny side to silly situations as she did.

By the time Mike and the rest of the workmen left each evening she usually just fell into bed and dropped off to sleep immediately.

The days passed chaotically but happily. Rosie was a frequent visitor and was a huge supporter of her plans for a gallery.

'It's a shame it's not nearer Stourton but, my goodness, it will be lovely when it's finished,' she enthused. 'It's also a shame you're going to miss the summer season, so we'll have to think of something clever to bring in the customers when you do open.'

'I've been thinking about that,' agreed Eleanor. 'I don't think we'll be ready to open until the end of August, so I was thinking of having a grand opening on the Bank Holiday. What do you think?'

'Not such a good idea,' Rosie warned. 'That's the date of the annual Stourton Festival and you don't want to cross swords with the Festival Committee. How about something to do with Harvest Festival?'

'Or the Autumn Equinox?' suggested Eleanor. 'I'll have a think about it.'

The days were long and hot, especially with all the dust that was flying around, and Eleanor left the house in Mike's capable hands when there was major work going on.

When the major carpentry work in the gallery started she took the opportunity to visit some local artists to get them on board with the gallery idea and to see if they would exhibit with her. She usually asked Rosie to go with her on these visits, but Rosie's husband Daniel had just come home from an extended visit to Hong Kong and they had taken a week's holiday together.

The afternoon was a success, and she had arranged for three lady artists friends of Rosie's to come and see the gallery the following Sunday, hoping enough renovation work would have been completed for them to see how it would look when it was finished.

She drove home in high spirits, loving the way the trees met overhead to make a green tunnel of the laneways. When she passed the fields of wheat, she noticed that the edges, although trimmed by the farmer, were still a riot of wildflowers that had been driven to the edges by the use of pesticides and week-killers. Poppies grew in abundance, showing in relief against the golden stems of escaped wheat, and lace-topped cow parsley.

Where the hedgerow trees had begun to reassert themselves, they were over-run with dog roses and Virginia creeper. The heavy sprays of elderflower had dropped and were now being replaced by the luscious black-red of the elderberries themselves. Eleanor thought about elderberry wine and wondered if the farm shop further down the road stocked a local brand.

As she pulled in behind Mike's van her heart sank at the sight of Justin's car parked next to it. Somehow the sight of an Alfa Romeo next to Mike's dented van looked out-of-place and vaguely vulgar. Getting out of the car she could hear Mike's voice from an upstairs window saying 'I'm sorry, young man, but I can't allow you to do that.'

As she came through the front door she glanced into the gallery and was astonished to see Nick Preston looking back at her. She was about to speak to him, when she heard more commotion from upstairs.

'Now look here. I don't know who you are. You can't just come in here and make yourself at home.' Mike was slightly shorter than average, but had a builder's physique and was not a man to be crossed. She could hear the warning notes in his voice, which Justin apparently could not.

'Oh, for God's sake, I *know* her!' came Justin's reply. Eleanor recognised that tone as well and knew that Justin's face would have turned red by now. He didn't like to be crossed.

Mike was not to be swayed, 'And I know the Queen, but I don't go round to her house unannounced and make myself at home in her bedroom.' There was an uncomfortable silence, and the men had obviously reached a stalemate, neither willing to back down.

Eleanor broke eye contact with Nick and ran up the stairs, trying to piece together what had happened. Justin had obviously rubbed Mike up the wrong way by turning up out of the blue, but what was Nick doing here?

'Oh there you are!' said Justin as soon as he saw her. She was dressed in a tunic top and leggings teamed with flat pixie boots, and he seemed about to pass a comment on that before continuing, 'Tell your *workman* that I'm your boyfriend and have every right to be here.' He raised his chin and smirked at Mike, waiting for Eleanor to back him up.

Eleanor, however, hesitated. She didn't want to have an argument with Mike, but she didn't want Justin to think that he could just walk into her new life. It felt like he was contaminating it with parts of her old life that she didn't really want to remember.

'I'm sorry, Mike,' she said, 'I didn't know he was coming. But I do know him. I'm sorry if he's been getting in your way.' She raised her eyebrows with what she hoped was a look of conspiracy, expecting that Mike would see that she thought Justin was the idiot and that she would talk to him later. He shrugged and walked back downstairs, humming and knocking his screwdriver against the wall as he went. She knew that this wasn't the end of the matter.

She walked over to Justin. 'What are you doing here?' she hissed, her face much closer to his than she had intended.

'I wanted to see what life was like in the country and how you were getting on without fibre optic broadband and Pret lunches.' He looked down at her with a superior expression on his face, obviously expecting her to be embarrassed that he had caught he out.

Eleanor had never seen him like this before. She knew that he didn't like the rural life, but she had never seen him so openly hostile.

'Is that your new boyfriend downstairs, then? He seems awfully protective of you. For a yokel.'

Eleanor stared. 'What? Who?'

It suddenly dawned on her that he was talking about Nick and she realised that she didn't even know what Nick was doing in the house, let alone what he might be saying anything that would lead Justin to think they were going out together.

'OK.' She thought quickly. 'Go and make a cup of coffee. These stairs will take you down to the kitchen. I'll be there in a minute.' She opened a door neatly concealed in the panelling and almost pushed him into the stair-well, despite his protestations. 'Careful, it's a bit dark.'

She walked back down the main stairs to find Nick, who was laying out some wooden planks on a trestle table. Glancing around, she saw that the room was almost completed. The walls had been painted a very pale cream and the unstained wood was being waxed as she watched. The carpet, although covered at the moment by plastic sheeting was a rich, dark maroon, that spoke of country houses and old money. She had managed to find a commercial quality one that was nevertheless deep and thick enough to seem luxurious.

'Do you want to tell me what's going on here?' she asked Nick, standing before him with her hands on her hips.

Nick laid down his tools and looked up unhurriedly. His baggy trousers and faded black t-shirt were obviously his work wear, and had seen better days, but he was one of those men who made any clothes look good. At that moment, she couldn't imagine him wearing anything else. The lock of hair that had drawn her attention previously still fell forwards over his face and she had the same urge to move it. The urge was countered by her anger at being put into an uncomfortable position, which she proceeded to vent on everyone in the room.

'For goodness sake, will you all stop staring and get on with whatever it is that you're meant to be doing.' She kicked at a pile of tins and offcuts of wood. 'And move this blasted stuff out of the way so that I can get through without falling over it. Mike, what's this man doing in my house? You know you're not meant to employ anybody else without my say-so. Come and have a word with me and tell me what's going on.'

Before Mike had a chance to answer she strode off to the kitchen where Justin was waiting with a steaming cup of coffee. He lay on one of the large leather sofas she had bought at a house sale, his long legs resting on the arm. He held out a cup of coffee for her.

'I couldn't find the vanilla syrup,' he said sweetly. 'Can't you get it out here?'

Eleanor felt like throwing the coffee back at him. How had she missed the fact that he was so arrogant before? She had taken his rudeness to others as a bit of a joke in the past, laughing when he had teased shop girls and taxi drivers, but now he was attacking those she had come to know well she saw how offensive he was being.

'Justin, I don't think this is a good idea,' she started, but she didn't finish the sentence, as Justin stood up and took the coffee from her hands, placing it on the work surface. He grabbed her hands, wrapped her arms around his neck and leant forward to kiss her. She pulled back and as she did so, stumbled into Nick, who was standing in the doorway.

He raised his eyebrows sardonically. 'Sorry, Miss,' he said, playing on the fact that Justin had called him a yokel, "I just came to apologise. I'll be leaving now, and I'm sorry if I offended you or your ... visitor.' Her turned and left as quickly as he had come.

Eleanor was dumbfounded. She had caught the sarcasm in his tone, but it didn't change the fact that he was leaving. For some reason, this seemed like the very last thing she wanted to happen.

'Justin!' she shouted in frustration, turning away from Nick.

'What have I done?'

'Just... You...Oh, just go away. This was a really bad idea, you coming down here. Please, just go back to the hotel. I'll meet you there for dinner.'

'But I haven't booked into the hotel. I thought I'd be staying here.' He had raised his voice to be sure that Nick heard and understood the implications. He turned his head to look after Nick and then looked back at Eleanor. He hesitated for a moment, then grabbed the jacket he had thrown over the back of the sofa. 'Actually, I think I've seen enough of Kent for now. I'll call you.'

Eleanor heard to the crunch of gravel as Justin's car pulled out of the drive and listened to the sound of his engine as it roared off down the lane until she could hear it no more. She found that she was more sorry that Nick had left than Justin.

As she sat cradling her cup of coffee, trying to make sense of what had just happened, Mike came into the room and stood for a moment looking at her.

'Mind if I make myself a cup of coffee?' he asked, picking up a mug from the draining board and holding it up.

'No, of course not,' she sighed, 'I think I've made a bit of a fool of myself today. You'd better get the biscuits as well.' She pointed to a tin labelled CAKE next to the sink.

'Don't worry about it. We see a lot worse than that in our line of work,' Mike grinned. 'I even saw a naked man chasing his wife's lover down the drive once!'

Eleanor laughed at the joke and relaxed a bit, sitting down at the large pine table. She loved the fact that it was an antique and had been used in the kitchens of one of the large country houses in Kent. What history it must have seen!

'Why was Nick Preston here?' she asked, taking a custard cream from the packet.

Mike brought his coffee over and sat with her. 'He came to get some wood from the stables and when I saw him I realised he'd be the perfect chap for the woodwork in your gallery. You know he's a carpenter, don't you?' Eleanor shook her head.

'He makes bespoke kitchen and bedroom furniture.' Mike continued. 'His workshop's at the back of his Mum's place: Stourton Hall Farm. He's built up a nice little business for himself and helps his parents run the farm at the same time.'

Eleanor had heard about the business from Rosie, but she hadn't realised that it belonged to Nick. Well, she'd made even more of a fool of herself than she'd thought.

'Can you apologise to him for me?' she asked.

'I can, but I don't know if he'll accept it. He doesn't *need* the work - he was just doing it as a favour to me.' Mike looked as if he would like to help her, and patted her hand. 'I'll try.'

Eleanor groaned. 'I was having a great day up until now. Now it's hot and sticky and I know I'm not going to get any sleep tonight if it doesn't cool down and on top of that, this has happened.' She put her head on her arms and felt like falling asleep and hoping it would all go away.

'Why don't you take a run down to the sea and forget about all this for a while,' Mike suggested, 'and we'll see what happens tomorrow. Have you been to Whitstable? You might be able to find some more artists who are interested in working with you.'

Eleanor took his suggestion, and left him to get on with his work while she drove to Whitstable for the afternoon.

It was a beautiful blustery day and she stood on the sea wall and let the wind blow her worries away. It whipped her hair into her eyes and left salt spray on her lips. Eleanor Stratton the personal shopper would have hated it. Eleanor Stratton from The Black Cat Gallery loved it.

She thought about her friends in London, and wondered what they would think of Whitstable. They would probably love the quirkiness of it, but she doubted they would last for long away from the bustle of the town. Lovely as it was for long weekends, visitors from 'the big smoke' soon got tired of the provincial nature of the town and returned to the bright city lights. She knew that Justin, in particular, would make fun of the size of the town and the lack of what he considered essential amenities.

She spent a happy couple of hours browsing through the little independent shops, then bought herself some chips and sat on the sea wall to eat them. She walked along the boardwalk to the harbour, and came across an artists' village where she took some photographs and made a few new contacts before driving home through the country lanes, relaxed and feeling a lot more positive.

Chapter Six

As the warm sun of July intensified into the hot glare of August, the gallery began to take shape. All building regulations had been complied with, the decorating had been completed as Eleanor had envisaged, and signs were going up at the end of the driveway. She had made a deal with a local sign writer to display adverts for his business at the gallery in exchange for a very good price for the Black Cat signs. The sign looked professional and yet inviting and the picture of the black cat looked so much like the cat at the gallery that Eleanor wondered if he had been the inspiration.

The problem that was now looming on the horizon was the sticky problem of cash flow. Almost all Eleanor's savings had been spent on getting the gallery up to scratch, and she had very little left over for her own part of the house. Not that it mattered much to her, as the gallery was her life. She woke up thinking about it, worked on it all day, and then went to bed thinking about it. It had become more than an obsession; it was as if it was an integral part of her now.

She was also very aware that time was ticking away. She had given herself a one month deadline for opening the gallery, which was now just over two weeks away. The next day she spoke to Mike as soon as he came on site.

'Mike, can I have a word?'

'Ooh, looks serious,' he joked, 'You're not giving me the sack are you?'

'No,' she smiled, leading him into the kitchen, 'But I do need to talk about something to do with work.'

Mike's face hardened. He knew that his men had been doing a good job on the gallery, and were on track to complete the work to schedule.

'What's the problem?'

'Well, the problem is mine, really. What's the chances of you having everything finished in ten days?'

Mike almost spat out his tea, 'You're joking, right?' He could see in her face that she wasn't.

Eleanor explained the reasons for asking him to complete the job earlier than expected, and he rubbed his stubbly chin with one hand.

'Well, I suppose it can be done...' he mused, 'Do you want me to get more people in, and do the job to the original specification – which will cost more – or cut back on what we do?'

'I hadn't thought about that,' Eleanor sighed, 'I suppose you'd better get more people in. We spent a long time going over those plans, and I wasn't asking for anything I didn't need.'

She leant over and pecked him on the cheek, patting his hand fondly. 'Thanks, Mike; I knew I could depend on you.'

The eponymous black cat had been a silent witness to the whole refurbishment process, popping up in the most unexpected places. Eleanor might find him on her bed in the middle of the day, or look out of the window to see him sauntering across to one of the stables. Only very rarely did he venture into the gallery when the workmen were there, but she would very often find him sitting on a window sill in the evening, looking out of the front window as if waiting for his owner to come home.

Sometimes she would join him, and look out through the leaded lights at the countryside, watching the bees in the honeysuckle and the butterflies in the buddleia. When she went upstairs and looked out of the upstairs windows she could see the changes in the countryside as the wheat ripened and turned to a darker shade of gold. The fields which had been planted with hay were cut, and bales dotted the furrows, waiting to be collected. It all gave Eleanor a sense of satisfaction as if a weight had been lifted off her shoulders. Without consciously knowing it, she seemed to have absorbed some of the collective consciousness of the farmers in the area, worrying about the crops and feeling relief when the harvest was gathered in.

She thought about naming the cat, but she never fed him and was conscious that he had a proper owner somewhere, who had already given him a name. One day she would find out what it was, but until then she would continue to call him 'Cat'.

As the middle of the month came ever closer, Eleanor began to think about advertising the gallery more aggressively. The signs outside were all very well, but in order to see them people needed to be passing by. She designed a poster, made a list of places that she might put them and rang the local newspaper.

Having set up an interview with a reporter for the next day, she rang Rosie and invited her for dinner, asking her to bring some of her pottery to display in the gallery.

Rosie's husband was away again, and she was glad of a chance to catch up with Eleanor. She arrived just as the workmen were leaving, almost tripping over as she fell out of her battered car, pulling an outsized patchwork bag behind her. She opened the boot and stacked a pile of plastic boxed in the entrance hall. Each box had an intriguing array of coloured packaging materials sticking out from all angles.

'All right, Mike?' she asked the foreman as she passed him in the dingy hallway, 'Have you forgotten me that soon?' Mike looked up from the work schedule he was carrying and soon recognised her.

They hugged, and exchanged pleasantries and Rosie told her friend that Mike had done the conversion work on her current home. While they were catching up, Eleanor took the opportunity to prepare the vegetables for dinner and put the kettle on.

They said goodbye to Mike and went see if it was warm enough to sit outside. It was, and they dragged two of the battered old easy chairs out into the courtyard. The overblown roses made a perfect backdrop to the cream tea presented on a pretty Poole Pottery tea set that Eleanor had picked up at a house sale. The cat came and sat near them, hoping for some clotted cream. He wasn't disappointed.

As the sun moved across the sky and the courtyard garden fell into shadow, and the two women moved into the huge old kitchen, each taking one end of the sofa. Eleanor

43

had added a few decorative touches to further improve what she called the 'olde worlde' charm of the place. There were now crocheted blankets on the sofas, a basket of logs by the Aga and a row of fresh hops tacked to the rafters. She spent some time discussing her design ideas with Rosie before talk turned to their hopes for the future.

'Daniel's going to be retiring soon and we'd love to run a Bed and Breakfast,' Rosie explained to Eleanor, 'It's a shame that our house is too small, so Mike's going over some plans with us to see if we can have an extension added.'

'Would you think about buying a different property?' asked Eleanor. She propped herself up on the arm of the sofa with her legs tucked under her to make room for the cat. She was one of those people who seem able to make themselves comfortable wherever they are.

'We'd love to, and with Daniel's pension, money won't be a problem. It's just that there aren't any suitable properties in the area.'

Eleanor sympathised with her friend, but could offer no suggestions.

They sat in silence for a while, sipping a second cup of tea, then talk turned to the gallery and what it would look like when it was filled with work.

'I'm so glad you didn't go with all that white you wanted,' Rosie commented, 'Minimalist is all right in the city, but not down here in the country. People want to find something that's rustic and charming, not something they can get anywhere else.'

'You're right, and I have to thank you for pointing that out to me at the beginning,' Eleanor smiled, stroking the cat absent-mindedly, 'I can't believe I'm such a novice at this! It all seemed so straight forward when I was planning it.'

Rosie smiled, 'Don't worry. You'll get there,' she predicted.

When they had finished their tea, they went through to the gallery and put Rosie's pottery on the shelving units that had been erected along part of the gallery's back wall. The natural colour of the wood was a perfect backdrop to the muted shades of the pieces that Rosie had brought over. Humble as she was about her own achievements, she seemed pleased with the effect they made when displayed in a gallery situation.

'Did Nick Preston do these for you?' asked Rosie as she ran her fingers along some particularly nice moulding.

'No,' said Eleanor shortly, 'A chap in Mike's team made it from a length of reclaimed timber he found out the back.'

Rosie heard the tone and refrained from asking more, but she made a mental note to ask Mike what was going on between Nick and Eleanor the next time she saw him.

'So tell me some more about this Bed and Breakfast.' Eleanor deftly changed the subject to one she knew Rosie would be keen to talk about. 'I thought you had your hands full with the shop.'

'You're right, it does take up a lot of my time, but Daniel's going to be retiring soon and we want something we can do together,' she pushed her hair out of her face, 'As much as he supports what I do in the shop, it's not really his 'thing'. He does like the idea of running a Bed and Breakfast place, though, and it's something we can both do together.'

She looked round the room, as if assessing its size.

'Our house just isn't big enough. You could fit the whole of our downstairs living space in your kitchen.'

Eleanor smiled, thinking about the chaotic jumble of Rosie's shop.

'You live in New Street, don't you? Is yours one with the plant pots outside?'

Rosie looked surprised. 'I thought you knew where I lived!' she exclaimed. 'Haven't you ever been to my house?'

'I always come to the shop when I want to see you, or you come here.'

'Well, in that case, I formally invite you to dinner on Thursday. You can poke around and make comments about it like I do about the this place!' she thought for a moment, 'and you can see my studio.'

At this point in the conversation, they both turned to the window at the same time. They had both heard the sounds of a bicycle being wheeled across the gravel and were looking out to see who it was. The sign at the entrance made it clear that the gallery wasn't open yet, so it couldn't be a customer.

Rosie jumped up and went to open the front door. 'What on earth is Audrey doing all the way out here?' she asked in amazement. 'Come on in, Audrey,' she called, 'and have a cup of tea.'

She turned to Eleanor, pushing her hair out of her eyes, and said 'That's all right isn't it? She's come an awfully long way on that bike.'

Audrey parked her bicycle and loped into the gallery, looking like a character from an Enid Blyton novel. She was someone who might be described as 'a handsome woman', with short salt-and-pepper hair and a no-nonsense approach to her that put many people's backs up. Eleanor and Rosie were both more than happy to deal with someone who could be trusted to be truly honest. Eleanor knew immediately that she was going to like this lady.

'Ms Stratton?' asked the newcomer, 'I do apologise for the intrusion, but when you hear why I'm here, I'm sure you'll forgive me.'

'You're very welcome,' replied Eleanor, Tea?' she offered, half expecting the visitor to ask for ginger beer instead.

'Gosh, yes!' exclaimed her guest. 'Splendid!'

Audrey looked around the galley and then glanced back out of the door as if she thought she might have wandered into the wrong house. 'Golly, this looks marvellous! I didn't expect it to be like this.'

'What did you expect it to be like?' laughed Eleanor, a reply which seemed to make her guest feel uncomfortable.

'Oh, you know, it's just that, well, people have been saying...' she started, looking round the room as if for inspiration. 'Oh look, there's my cat, Darwin!'

This turn of events surprised everybody. Audrey called to the cat, which trotted over to her like an obedient puppy. She picked it up and took it outside to her bicycle

46

basket, which upon closer inspection was merely a cat basket strapped between the handlebars. The cat seemed happy enough to be put inside and submitted without complaint when the lid was buckled up over its head.

'I'm going to have to take a rain cheque on that cup of tea,' she said 'Bye now!' And she pedalled off down the lane as fast as she had come.

Eleanor and Rosie looked at each other and burst into giggles.

'Oh, my goodness!' exclaimed Eleanor, 'Does she always do that?'

'Do what?'

'Breeze in like a dose of salts and rush off mid-sentence?'

Rosie thought for a moment, 'I don't know about always, but quite a lot of the time.'

Their laughter intensified as they went over the encounter, and they ended up with tears rolling down their cheeks.

'Oh, I really needed that!' said Eleanor when they had calmed down. 'Let me just check on the dinner and you can tell me who she is.'

Rosie pushed her hair back, settled comfortably into her place on the sofa and told Eleanor that Audrey was the local equivalent of an eccentric millionaire. Devoted to her cats, she had never had to work, but spent her time doing good works on a variety of committees in Stourton. A string of husbands had left her richer than ever but with no children. She lived on the other side of Stourton, and Eleanor said she was surprised that she had come so far on her bicycle to find him.

'Oh, she'd cycle to John O'Groats to find Darwin if she had to,' Rosie's face softened, 'Those cats are like her babies.'

'And what was that about the gallery not being what she expected?' Eleanor asked. As the gallery was still not open, she was at a loss to understand how people could have misconceptions about it.

'Well, there has been some local speculation about what you're doing up here,' said Rosie carefully, 'There are a lot of ladies in Stourton who feel that they should have been included in your plans just by virtue of their seniority. They're like a sort of unofficial village council.'

'Oh, no!' cried Eleanor. 'I never even thought about that. I was so wrapped up in what I was doing that I didn't even consider which other people might need to be involved. What do you think I should do about it?'

Rosie thought for a moment. 'Did you say that the press were coming to talk to you?' Eleanor nodded confirmation. 'Then why don't you put them off for a week and invite the local would-be-goods to a pre-opening soiree on the same day. If you can butter them up and get them all on board it will make your life a whole lot easier, I can tell you.'

Chapter Seven

The following Thursday, Eleanor drove into Stourton and parked in the little car park behind the church. Walking through the narrow streets towards Rosie's house, she once again thought about how lovely it must be to live in a town where everyone knew each other. After all, with the houses facing directly onto the pavements, and with no front gardens, it was hard not to know your neighbour.

The road in which Rosie lived was called New Street, but looked as if it had been built by the Victorians. Matching rows of whitewashed cottages faced each other across tiny pavements that lived up to their name by being paved with stone flags. No tarmac or concrete here.

Each home owner had managed to put their own stamp of individuality on their property, either by painting the front door, adding shutters, putting quirky items in the window or by some other means.

Rosie's house was easily identifiable as the woodwork was all painted in the same shade of lavender blue as her current range of pottery. Her net curtains were made of real lace, and she had created a large pottery plaque which had been mounted over the front door announcing 'Rosie and Daniel, pots and plans'.

The inside of the cottage was a surprise to Eleanor. Daniel had obviously had more of a say in the decorating than Eleanor would have expected. Everywhere was immaculately tidy and beautifully clean. The tiny interior was decorated in a neutral colour scheme which was livened up with splashes of colour introduced by rows of colourful artwork on the walls, throws and cushions in painted silks, and a Tiffany-style lampshade.

'This is lovely,' called Eleanor to Rosie who had gone through a stable door to make tea in the kitchen.

'I know,' laughed Rosie, 'Daniel can't work if it's in a mess, and I actually find it rather calming as well. After all the chaos of the shop, I find I can come home and chill out here. I love it.'

She brought Eleanor a mug of tea, and showed her around the rest of the house, before taking her back downstairs. They put the mugs in the kitchen and Eleanor looked out of the back window.

The back garden was only as wide as the house but it seemed to go on for ever. A stone-flagged patio area with cast-iron furniture was ringed with plants in pots of all sizes. A large chiminea stood to one side, and looked as if it was well-used in the summer months. Rosie saw her looking at it.

'We use that all the time when the weather's good enough. You'll have to come to our next dinner party. Now, come and see the studio.'

They walked down a gravel path edged with Victorian terracotta tiles to the bottom of the garden where Rosie had her studio. The flowers bed were overflowing with plants of all kinds, pushing their way through on the path and peeping through behind one another.

'It's all rather higgledy-piggledy,' said Rosie, picking the heads off some roses as she passed, 'but I like the old-fashioned cottage garden style.' She leant over to pick a handful of late strawberries and passed some to Eleanor, 'This bit here is my herb garden. The ones at the front are the ones I use all the time, and the big ones at the back are the ones that are mostly for show.'

The end of the garden was shielded from view by a tall wicker fence. Rosie pushed open a gate and stood back to let Eleanor see what was behind it.

'You see, it pays to have an architect for a husband,' she said, proudly.

Many artists have converted sheds in their gardens which they use as studio spaces, but this was completely different. Daniel had designed and built a log cabin with separate areas for the different types of work Rosie needed to do. A wall separated the kiln from the rest of the space, and Eleanor could see that a mezzanine floor area was used

50

for storage. It was beautifully constructed and perfect for Rosie.

The room was surprisingly well-ordered, with work-areas allocated for making, drying, glazing and firing the work. Eleanor wandered around, looking at the drawings Rosie was working on.

'Oh, these are nice,' she said, when she came across a design for plates with slip-trailed lettering around them, 'Could you do one like this for The Black Cat Gallery?'

'Flip over the page.'

She did so, and saw that Rosie had already sketched out the design for a plate with the name of the gallery around the outside and a picture of Darwin in the middle with the gallery in the background. The rich honey-colour of the lettering shone against the dark chocolate-brown of the under-glazing. As a piece it was at once contemporary and yet gave a distinctly overt nod towards past potters and their techniques.

'I was hoping to get it ready for the opening. It'll be a gift from one struggling artist business woman to another.'

Eleanor laughed, 'I'm not an artist!'

'Not exactly, but you're helping others to be, and that's just as important. Where would we be if we all sat at home creating stuff and there was nowhere to show it off or sell it?'

They wandered back to the house, and Rosie made another cup of tea. The conversation turned towards the Grand Opening of the gallery and the pre-opening party that was planned for the next day.

'I hope I've invited the right people,' worried Eleanor. 'I didn't want to invite exactly the same people as those that are coming to the Grand Opening.'

They went through the list together, and Rosie put Eleanor's mind at rest. She had done the best that could be done. They had organised afternoon tea, weeded the garden around the car park, and re-designed the seating area in the conservatory so that people could take their tea indoors.

Eleanor had even hired some pretty vintage china for the event.

As the light began to fade, Rosie invited Eleanor to stay for dinner and the two friends settled in for the evening.

'I can't stay too late,' said Eleanor, 'I don't think there's anything else left to do, but I want to check the phone for messages, and give myself time to sort out anything that has gone wrong while I've been out enjoying myself!'

'Don't be so hard on yourself; you've done a great job.'

'Really? Sometimes it feels as if I'm swimming against the tide, as they say.'

While Rosie prepared the meal, Eleanor looked at the family photos in the living room. They were mostly ones from recent years, showing Daniel and Rosie at various holiday destinations.

Eleanor picked up one of a little girl about six years old with flaming red hair the same as Rosie's. The light was behind her, and her hair floated round her head like a halo. With her big grin and freckled nose, she looked like the archetypal Annie actress. Eleanor picked up the photo.

'Is this little girl a relation?' she asked, 'She looks a lot like you.'

The chopping noises from the kitchen stopped, and Eleanor walked through to see why. Rosie was standing at the counter with the knife still in her hand, staring off into space.

'Rosie? Are you alright?'

Rosie turned round quickly 'Yes, I'm fine,' she pushed the hair out of her face and continued, 'She's my niece, and her name's Elizabeth. I looked after her for a while when she was younger, when her mother was ill, but I don't see her anymore.'

Eleanor waited to see if the story would be continued, but Rosie resumed her chopping and said no more.

'You know, if you want to talk about anything, I'm always just on the end of the phone,' she said.

Rosie turned and gave her a quick hug.

'I do know that. But there's no mystery. She lived with me when I was married to my first husband. Her mother was his sister, so she's not a blood relation although she does look a lot like me. As I said, her mother was ill for a long time and it seemed like a better idea for her to have a home with us. When her mother got better, she went back to live with her again, and when I got divorced we lost touch.' She laughed, ruefully, 'The family never did like me much. I was rather too much of a free spirit for them. I have a suspicion that they deliberately kept Libby from contacting me. Like I said, I got divorced from Stephen, so I effectively divorced myself from the rest of his family as well.'

'Oh, I am sorry,' was all Eleanor could think to say. She wondered why Rosie had not gone on to have children of her own, but was wary of prying. One day, Rosie might tell her, and if she never found out, well, it was none of her business. She knew Rosie and Daniel had married when Daniel was already quite old, so perhaps that was the reason. Perhaps she would never know.

Over dinner, the women talked about friends in Stourton and Eleanor plucked up courage to ask about Nick Preston.

'Oh, he's a bit of a celebrity round here, I think,' Rosie told her, 'From what I can gather he was the golden child in the family, the boy all the girls wanted to go out with in school, and now he's the last hope for the family dynasty in Stourton.'

'So the family's lived her for a long time, then?'

'I'm not really a local history fan, and I try not to listen to gossip, but from what I can gather, they've been the big fish round here since medieval times.'

'So Daddy's the local squire-slash-landlord and he's the dashing Prince Charming? No wonder he's so unbearable. He must think all the girls are just falling over him.' Eleanor thought how she, too, was beginning to fall for his charms.

'Well, there's a lot of pressure on the lad, don't forget. I think he's quite shy and yet everyone expects him to sweep girls off their feet like Colin Firth playing Mr Darcy.'

Rosie started to clear the plates away and Eleanor stood up to help her.

'Anyway, why all the interest in Nick Preston?' She looked closely at Eleanor, 'You're not falling for him yourself are you?'

'Goodness, no!' said Eleanor, a little too quickly. 'I hardly even know the man,' and she quickly changed the subject.

At the end of the evening, Eleanor bid her friend goodbye and drove back to the gallery. She was at last beginning to get used to the narrow, unlit roads and the fact that she had to pull over into a passing-place each time she met an oncoming car. The light was beginning to fade as she drew into the car park of The Black Cat Gallery, and as she crunched across the gravel she shivered. The house took on a brooding look in the half-light and she decided that she needed to buy a timer switch for some of the lamps in the living room. At least it would be more welcoming to come home to than a huge silent building. This building was a place for the whole community to meet, not just for one person. Hopefully, the days when it was filled with laughter would be recreated in the days to come.

Chapter Eight

Eleanor woke early on the day of the pre-opening party. The dawn chorus was still chirping away outside her bedroom window and she could feel that the sun would be high and hot by the afternoon.

Hoping to calm down a little, she decided to go for a walk while it was still cool, so she dressed in several layers, choosing a strappy top, a tunic and a cardigan, thinking that she could peel off the layers if she needed to. Grabbing her camera, she struck off across the fields. Drops of dew still clung to the grass, wetting her legs as she passed. She loved the early morning and had worked out a little route for herself that took her down one side of the valley, along beside the river for a short while and then up a long but gentle hill back to the end of her lane.

Every time she followed this route she found something else to look at. When she had lived in town, the seasons had seemed to pass by marked only by the numbers on the calendar. Out here in the country she could see the trees and flowers change as weeks went past. Some early blackberries were beginning to ripen, their delicate blossom long gone, and she could even hear that the bird songs were different at different times of day. She repeatedly told herself that she must make an effort learn the names of the different birds if this was to be her permanent home.

Today was not a day for listening to the thoughts that were running through her head, though. This was a morning for relaxation, so she could be ready for the afternoon ahead. She hummed as she walked, swishing her hands along the cow parsley that lined the verges, listening out for any cars that might come racing around the corners. Taking a stroll in the countryside was not the carefree, leisurely activity it used to be.

As she walked she started to wonder which route Nick Preston had taken on the first day she had met him, when she had seen him cutting across the fields. She had looked at it earlier, and it had been signposted as a Public Footpath, although it was overgrown with nettles at the moment. She decided that she would choose that path when she went for a walk in the autumn, after the nettles had died down.

Even as she was thinking this, she heard a whistle and a Springer spaniel came bounding through the hedge towards her. Startled, she put up her hands to defend herself and took a step backwards, away from the animal.

The dog, however, came to a halt in front of her and looked as startled as she was to find someone in her way. It was a large dog for its breed, with attractive black and grey markings. Despite the wary look on its face, it's tail wagged and it seemed to be friendly.

'Bracken!' called a voice Eleanor recognised, and her heart sank.

'Go!' she whispered to the dog, urgently. 'Get back to your master!' The dog didn't move, and in a few moments, Nick Preston leapt over a five-barred gate leading through the hedge to the field beyond.

He stopped when he saw Eleanor and looked back up the road as if expecting to see someone else. His hair was tousled as if he had just got out of bed, which he might well have done this early in the morning, and her heart skipped a beat as she looked at him. His face was still unshaven and she caught herself wondering how it would feel if she ran her fingers along his jawbone.

'Are you on your own?' he asked.

'Yes,' She replied, cagily, hoping he could not read the thoughts that were running through her mind. 'I'm taking a walk.' She put her hand to her own hair to smooth it down and she wondered briefly what she looked like in her jeans and wellingtons. As he continued to look at her without speaking, she continued, 'You seem to be out for a walk yourself.' It was a stupid attempt at conversation, and she racked her brains for something more interesting to say.

'That's right,' he confirmed, lifting up a basket to show her. 'I was out collecting mushrooms. What are you doing?'

'Nothing. Just walking.' She was beginning to wonder why he was asking her these questions. All she was doing was taking a walk, and that fact that he had stopped her was not only annoying, but he had compounded his error by making her feel uncomfortable.

'I'll leave you to it, then,' he said, and whistling to his dog, he jumped back over the gate and was gone. Eleanor started to speak, but it was too late. All that was left was a footprint in the mud and a flurry of insects that rose from waving grasses.

Making her way back to the gallery, Eleanor thought about Nick and why it was that they two of them seemed unable to communicate. He was very good-looking, but it seemed he had very few social skills. She remembered that she had been going to ask Perhaps he was just one of those men who lived their lives at odds with the world and never managed to settle down to a permanent relationship. His brusque manner certainly seemed to indicate that he might be.

By lunch time, what little composure she had built up during her walk had completely disappeared. She was worried about the way the gallery looked, about the parking, about whether people would like the brand of tea she had chosen, about whether the press would turn up and most of all what people would think of the gallery. She dressed with care in a floral tea-dress and matching cardigan, then changed into a blouse and skirt before finally settling on a pair of wide-legged trousers paired with a floaty top.

At a little after two o'clock, however, people were starting to arrive, and they all seemed to be very impressed with what she had done, although she thought she could hear one or two reservations in the comments they made. Most of the negative comments seemed to be minor points, and centred around the lack of consultation that had been done prior to the alterations.

Rosie had come along to help serve tea and greet the guests, while her friend Jan looked after the shop for a couple of hours. Eleanor hoped that having a local face involved in the gallery would help people to accept her as part of the business community. They managed to find time for a quick chat while they grabbed a quick cup of tea in the kitchen and did some washing-up.

'Mrs Ransley was telling her cronies that she hadn't heard about the gallery until she got your invitation to this,' Rosie reported, 'She seemed to think you should have asked around before deciding to open a gallery in their village.'

'Well, I consulted with the owner, Mrs Wilkinson, about all the alterations,' replied Eleanor, 'so I can't see what they have to moan about. It's not really any of their business…is it?'

A knowing look came over Rosie's face. 'I think there are a lot of people round here who think that *everything* is their business,' she said.

Eleanor had invited everyone she could think of who might have an interest in what she was doing with the gallery, from the Mayor and the shopkeepers to the headmistress of Stourton Primary School and the committee of the WI. She made a point of taking the time to speak to each of them in turn, trying to find out what is was that their particular group might want from the gallery.

'Can I introduce myself?' she asked the Mayor, politely, 'I'm Eleanor Stratton. What do you think about the gallery?'

The Mayor shook her hand and introduced her to his wife, who seemed to take the role of Mayor's consort very seriously.

'Yes, yes,' mumbled the Mayor, vaguely, 'It all seems very nice. Lovely cakes.' He took another bite of his almond slice, which effectively brought the conversation to a halt.

Eleanor smiled at the Lady Mayoress. 'I believe Rosie McAllister met you at the door. Do you know her? She runs the vintage shop in Market Street.'

The Lady Mayoress sniffed and told Eleanor that she usually avoided buying second-hand goods. Eleanor held back from pointing out the difference between vintage and second-hand goods or discussing the ecological benefits of recycling. Instead, she smiled and pointed to the lady's tea cup. 'More tea?'

She moved from group to group, but found that they were often talking about people and places she didn't know. She found that she was circling the room nodding and smiling at people without actually speaking to anyone in particular. On one occasion, the conversation in the group stalled altogether when she joined them, and she moved quickly away, making the excuse that she was needed in the kitchen.

One person who was notable by her absence was Audrey, although Eleanor supposed that she would come along to the official public opening. She had warmed to the lady and her quirky ways and hoped they would become friends in the future.

At around three o'clock, Eleanor noticed a small disturbance near the front door and went to investigate. The Mayor and his wife were standing by one of the larger paintings posing while the photographer from the local newspaper took some pictures.

Eleanor paused for a moment to think about what to do. Surely if it was her event, then she should be in the photograph, but on the other hand, if the event was going to be in the newspaper at all, then that was a bonus. Free advertising was never easy to come by.

In the end, she waited for the photographer to finish and then held out her hand to him.

'Hi,' she said, 'I'm Eleanor Stratton: this is my gallery. Can I ask who invited you today?'

The man was scribbling something in his notebook and then stuffed it into one of the many pockets in his cargo pants and turned to face her.

'Sorry, love?'

'I said, I'm the owner of this gallery and I asked who invited you to come to this event and take photographs.'

'Oh, I don't need an invite. I just follow Graham and Margaret and photograph whatever they do. I'm freelance, you see, but the paper's always happy to pay for a photo of The Mayor.'

'But you can't just come into my party and start taking photos.' Eleanor was becoming increasingly agitated by the exchange and could feel a subtle change to the atmosphere in the room as people heard the tone in her voice change. Guests were beginning to listen to what she was saying.

The man shrugged. 'Freedom of the press, love.'

Eleanor looked around, and knew that the very people she had invited to the party to win over were the ones who would defend the right of their Mayor to be photographed anywhere he wanted. They were the ones who would be reading the newspaper and see that he had been to the gallery. She drew a steadying breath.

'Oh, I didn't mean to offend you. I was just trying to find out what was going on. Can I get you a cup of tea?' She hoped that the offer would sound sincere, although she felt like she was speaking through gritted teeth.

As she waited for a reply, a tall, willowy girl with a Roman nose stepped forward. She held a reporter's notebook in her both hands and leant forward slightly as she spoke, like a crane about to spear a goldfish. Her tight dress only served to emphasise her slim figure.

'Everything all right, Nigel?' she asked the photographer, who shrugged noncommittally.

The girl turned to Eleanor and flashed a laminated press card. 'Lou Evans – Kentish Lifestyle' she said, curtly. 'Do you have a problem with us photographing the Mayor as he goes about his official duties?'

'No,' blurted out Eleanor, 'Not at all. It's just...I...I wondered who this man was.'

'Well I report on *everything* that goes on in Stourton. I am the Kentish Lifestyle area rep, and my readers always like to see pictures of their Mayor. He's quite a local celebrity, you know. Or perhaps you don't. You haven't lived here for long, have you?'

'Um, no. Look, would you like to sit down and do a proper interview with me?' Eleanor suddenly realised that she needed to get on the right side of this person. 'Any time at all.'

'It's OK,' the girl looked around the gallery, 'I've talked to a few people here and I think I've got everything I need.' She turned abruptly to speak to the photographer, and then just as speedily, strode out of the door on her long legs and was gone.

On the whole, though, the afternoon seemed to go well. Eleanor ended the afternoon with a short speech, thanking everyone for coming and letting them know the names of the first artists who would be exhibiting in the gallery. She spent the evening tidying up and by bedtime, she was ready to drop, and fell into bed with little thought of what was to come.

The bombshell came three days later when the local paper was delivered. The headline read 'NEW GALLERY OWNER SNUBS LOCAL ARTISTS'.

Chapter Nine

Eleanor's hands were shaking as she read the article and she found to her horror that it was even worse that it had seemed from the headline. They had included a photograph of her turning away from a well-known local artist. In reality, the lady had just excused herself, and Eleanor had turned to speak to someone else, but clever cropping made it look like a deliberate snub. The girl reporter had really gone to town on Eleanor's arrogant attitude and her dismissal of local talent. She might just be a young reporter trying to make a name for herself, but she was crucifying Eleanor in the process. Eleanor was furious with the reporter, but she also kicked herself for not insisting on a quick interview in person. She was sure she could have won the girl over and given her a positive story to print.

The breakfast things were pushed to one side, as Eleanor spread out the paper, looking from the picture on the front page to the main article on the following page.

The worst thing about the article was that many of the facts weren't even true. She wondered which guests the girl had spoken to, or if she had even spoken to anyone. Eleanor had agreed to take the work of two local artists and of course she had Rosie's work displayed with great prominence.

She tried to think about the old adage the 'All publicity is good publicity' but she was finding it hard to see how anything in this article could be turned to her advantage.

When Mike came round to pick up some tools, he found her still very upset from reading the newspaper report, and did the best that he could to cheer her up.

The official gallery opening was now set for the end of August and Eleanor's preparations now took up a lot more of her time.

She added miles to her car odometer by driving up and down the county visiting studios and workshops and picking up work. She now kept the back seats permanently lowered so that she could stack prints and paintings in the back.

When Mike had left, she took her bad mood out on the housework, vacuuming and dusting with vigour. When she had finished, she grabbed a quick cup of soup for lunch and taking her watercolours out in to the garden she began to sketch the roses.

A beautiful pink-edged old-fashioned rose had grown up against one of the stone walls, and with the afternoon sunlight slanting across it, presented a very pretty picture. Some of the blossoms had dropped and the hips were starting to form, but some blooms were still full and beautiful. There were even a few new buds forming, although they wouldn't necessarily make it to maturity if the weather turned. Eleanor rarely painted, but when she did, she found that it calmed her down. With long, languid strokes she blocked in the colours of the roses, not minding that some of the paint dripped and ran. She painted without thinking what she was doing and let the colours blend with each other as they touched.

While she waited for the paint to dry, she looked up at the clouds that scudded past and watched a pair of wagtails boldly pecking at the ground in front of her. A mountain ash leant over the wall and, although she had not recognised it before, the bright orange berries were now unmistakable. She relaxed, and as she enjoyed the peace of the afternoon an idea came to her.

A chance remark of Mike's about the local radio station had got her thinking, and Eleanor rang the local radio to ask how to go about getting some time on air. The receptionist told her that she could either buy advertising time or agree to be a guest on one of the shows. Booking an interview, Eleanor set about making notes for herself. This time she would make sure that the report went the way *she* wanted.

The interview was to be pre-recorded, and was done over the phone. Eleanor had spoken directly to the DJ who had interviewed to her before and convinced him that she had a great story.

The call went well. The DJ was happy to use the angle of misinterpretation to have a dig at his rival, the local newspaper and Eleanor came across as considerate, competent and approachable. She used the interview to publicise her Grand Opening and came away feeling much better about the whole situation. They had even laughed about the way she had chosen the name of the gallery, with the DJ commenting that she'd made friends with at least one local resident.

With the gallery ready, but not yet officially open, Eleanor found herself at a loose end. She had a week to spare and nothing urgent to do. After the hard work of the past two months, it was at the same time a relief and a puzzle. She wondered what she could do with herself. She had been so busy with the gallery since she had come to live in Kent that she had hardly had time to make any new friends, and found that her only true friend was Rosie.

Hoping that she would be run off her feet once the gallery opened, she decided to take a holiday and booked herself into a spa hotel for a four-day break.

She spent the time taking advantage of all the therapies on offer and when she returned, she was refreshed and felt able to take on anything that life could throw at her.

***

After a week of overcast skies, threatening rain at any moment, the day of the Grand Opening was mercifully dry and clear.

The fields around the gallery were turning from their bright summer green to the mellow gold of autumn with the fat green heads of wheat showing clearly against the yellowing stalks.. The laneway was not as overgrown as it had been now that the grass was beginning to die back and the car park area was spick and span. The whole countryside had taken on an atmosphere of quiet satisfaction as farmers brought in the harvest and could relax for a while. The bales

64

of straw and hay in the fields waiting to be taken to barns across the county were an indication of a good harvest.

Eleanor had put up posters advertising the opening everywhere she could think of. She had even asked Mike to make her some little wooden signs to put up at the side of the road, and they had now been up for a week.

The morning of the opening, she added balloons and streamers to the signs at the ends of the roads which led to the gallery and put up bunting around the car park. She hoped people would come. At least, she thought, she could rely on the artists and a few of their invited guests to turn up.

Fifteen minutes before the advertised start time, she heard a car pull into the car park. She pushed Darwin off her lap, brushed off the cat hairs and went to see who it was, her heart thumping. 'Please don't let it be that girl reporter,' she thought.

As the Grand Opening started, the car park began to fill up. Eleanor had put up trestle tables in the patio garden to serve refreshments and had put up PRIVATE signs on some of the doors to guide people through the gallery on their way to be served. She hoped that they would stop to look at the work on their way past and perhaps even stop to buy.

Eleanor had chosen a simple floral shift dress for the afternoon, and had thrown a cardigan around her shoulders. Her hair shone, and she had kept her make-up simple. She wanted to look capable and yet approachable and had spent a long time wondering what to wear. Her first instinct had been to wear something 'arty', but then realised that she should not try to be anything other than herself.

She stood at the front door to welcome her guests, giving each one a leaflet about the gallery and chatting briefly to as many as she could. Above the hubbub of chatter, she could hear Rosie's wicked chuckle.

Rosie had volunteered to sit in the gallery and take the money for any sales that were made and was in her element chatting to the guests. She was also ideally placed to be able to answer any questions about her own work. Although she was local, many people had not yet seen her work, and were surprised to find a potter in their midst.

About an hour into the event, Rosie came darting out of the gallery, one hand holding back her hair and the other clutching a watercolour painting.

'You don't take credit cards, do you?' she asked.

'Um, no,' replied Eleanor. ' Not yet. Why don't they just write a cheque?'

'Well, she's offered to, but I didn't know if we could accept one for £650 without knowing who they are.'

Eleanor grinned. 'That's fabulous. Can we find out who it is and get someone to vouch for them?'

At that moment, Eleanor's attention was caught by a movement at the far side of the car park and was annoyed to see Nick Preston appear out of the overgrown Public Footpath and walk straight towards the gallery. He waved to Audrey who had just parked her car and went to speak to her before taking her arm to walk her to the gallery.

They seemed to know each other well and Audrey leant into Nick as she walked. Eleanor wondered briefly what it would be like to have the support of such a strong, capable-looking escort. He certainly looked very different today in a well-cut suit and tie instead of his normal casual clothes. As they approached the entrance, Eleanor was at a loss over what she should say to him. After their last encounter there seemed very little left to talk about. She greeted Audrey who had dressed with her usual careful style and looked cool and elegant in a cream two-piece.

'You look nice today, Audrey,' Eleanor complimented her, 'Come to think of it, you always do!' She looked down ruefully at her own jeans and battered floral top, 'I really should take the time to dress up, I suppose. I used to dress properly every day when I was working in London, but nowadays I just throw on what's comfortable.'

'I think you look lovely, dear,' said Audrey, kindly, 'I sometimes wish I could dress more casually, but I just never seem to have the right clothes in my wardrobe!'

Eleanor smiled, 'I think we waste a lot of time wishing we could be someone else and we should really each stick with our own style.' She twiddled the buttons on her cardigan. 'Anyway, I'll be wearing my grown-up clothes every day once the gallery's up and running.'

She was saved from speaking to Nick at all, as it turned out, because a tall lady emerged from the house as he and Audrey approached.

'Hello, Audrey,' she enthused, greeting her friend with a kiss. 'Nicky, you're late. I thought we were going to meet at home first. I couldn't wait because I've got Bridge in half an hour, so we came without you.'

Eleanor's heart missed a beat as the lady leant forwards to move Nick's hair out of his eyes and patted him on the shoulder.

Turning to Eleanor she said, 'Thank you so much letting me have that picture. I've been after one of Graham's pieces for ages, and that view is just spectacular. Now Audrey's here she can vouch for me in person, so please don't worry about the money.'

As she spoke, Eleanor noticed that this lady's hair fell into her eyes in the same way that Nick's did. Taking in the lean frame and deep brown eyes, she realised that she was talking to Nick's mother.

'That's not a problem, Mrs Preston. I just didn't realise who you were at first.'

Nick hugged his mother briefly and had disappeared into the house before Eleanor had time to say more.

She was about to follow him when she heard a voice calling her name.

'Miss Stratton?'

She smiled, 'Call me Eleanor, please.'

'My name's Maisie and I'm here to write a report on the event for The East Kent Times, if that's all right with you?' The girl waved a reporter's notebook and smiled.

Eleanor's heart sank. Not another reporter. She looked again at the girl. This one was slightly older than the previous reporter, and seemed to be a lot friendlier. Her short curls bounced as she moved her head, constantly assessing the room and noticing everything that was going on.

'Of course. Would you like to come into the kitchen?'

'Actually, I wonder if we could just have a chat in the gallery as we wander around? Then I can ask about any of the work that I see, and I can get your immediate reaction. Would that be OK?'

Eleanor agreed, and followed her into the main gallery. She could see Nick a little further along, talking to his mother about one of the paintings, and had to drag her attention back to the reporter.

During the course of the interview, she was able to give a detailed account of why she wanted to start the gallery, how she had done it, and what sort of work she would be selling. The reporter seemed to be genuinely interested in the art work, and keen that the gallery should be a success. Eleanor was happy to open up to her and felt that this more open approach allowed her to put herself across in a much better light.

Keeping one eye on Nick, she showed the reporter the whole of the gallery, and discussed one or two of the artists in particular. The girl then pulled out a digital camera and asked for a photograph, which she quickly took herself.

By the time the interview had concluded, Nick and his mother had left, and Eleanor was called away to speak to another prospective exhibitor.

The afternoon got even busier and when the last people left it was getting on for six o'clock. She didn't see Nick again and guessed that he must have left via another footpath and not through the front entrance. She wondered if this was a deliberate choice so that he could avoid seeing her, or whether it was just coincidence.

'You again,' she said to Darwin when she went into the kitchen and noticed him curled up on the sofa, 'At least you like it here. I'd better ring Audrey and let her know you're staying the night.'

She stopped to pet him for a while, as much for her own benefit as for his.

'Do you think it went all right?' she asked him. Darwin purred and rolled over onto his back to expose his stomach for more scratching.

'You soppy old cat,' she said, scratching his ears as well as his tummy. 'Well, I think it went OK, even if you're not going to tell me what you thought. Everyone seemed to have a good time, and Maisie was a much nicer reporter than that other girl. Let's hope this means our luck has changed.'

She rang Audrey quickly, and when she got ready for bed she dropped off to sleep immediately, more relaxed than she had been for weeks.

***

Audrey became a regular visitor, sometimes bringing the black cat Darwin with her on her bike and sometimes coming alone to retrieve him from a cosy spot somewhere in the grounds of the gallery. She often stayed for tea, and stayed for a chat. She told Eleanor that she had been to Art College in Paris when she was younger, but that none of her husbands had understood or supported her passion and so it had dropped out of her life.

One afternoon, on a rare day of autumn sunshine, they sat in the garden to drink their tea, listening for the jangle of the gallery bell and talking about romance. The smell of the roses and the sound of the birdsong made a perfect backdrop for a conversation of this kind.

With forty years between them, the two women had grown up in completely different worlds and yet the process of falling in and out of love remained the same. They shared memories of unrequited love and of boys who had chased them even though they had no interest in a liaison.

As the afternoon progressed, they started to talk about 'the one that got away'.

'There was this one boy I dated years ago. It was just after I had left school,' Audrey told her, ' He was taller than me, which, let's face it, not may boys were, and so

69

handsome!' Her face softened as she spoke of him, 'We didn't have much money, but he used to take me to the pictures and to the coffee shop, and we had a great time. The only thing was, Daddy didn't approve, and in the end I felt I had to break it off.' She looked out of the window for a long minute or two, her eyes darting about as if searching for a memory.

'I can still remember the colour of his eyes and the sound of his voice, but I don't think I'd recognise him if I saw him now. It's funny, isn't it, the things we remember and those we forget?'

Eleanor listened quietly.

'Anyway, he left to go to Art College in London, and we lost touch. That was one of the things we had in common. We'd go sketching in the fields for hours at a time. He was so good it put my poor efforts to shame, but he was such a great teacher. Perhaps if we'd stayed together he might have taught me to be a proper artist instead of a Sunday afternoon painter.' She shook her head and smiled sadly.

'But I don't regret marrying Frank. Not for a moment. He was a Civil Servant, and I was proud to be his wife. How different that was from being the wife of a starving artist living in a garret! Perhaps Daddy was right: that probably wasn't the best life for me...'

Eleanor's heart went out to her, and she hoped that she herself would know love when it came to her and not throw away the chance of a lifetime.

'Anyway,' Audrey said, getting up from the chair and shaking out her skirts, 'This isn't going to buy the baby a new bonnet. I'll just get Darwin and then I'll be off.' She placed her cup carefully on the tea tray and went into the house.

Calling to her cat, she left quickly, leaving Eleanor to ponder on the wisdom of letting your parents choose a husband. Surely it was better to follow your heart, wherever it might lead?

Chapter Ten

After an initial flurry of sales at the opening, business at the gallery was slow and Eleanor realised that she would need to organise a series of special events to draw in visitors.

Her first one would be an Autumn Food Fair, she thought, imagining braziers of chestnuts, hot apple cider and marquees of local produce. She started to research what other people provided at their Autumn Fairs, and was pleased to find that her initial ideas had been spot on.

As she planned, getting quotes for marquees, and booking stallholders it occurred to her that it might be possible to develop the stable blocks. She would have to be careful about how much money she spent from now on, bearing in mind the short term of the tenancy, but it might be a worthwhile investment.

She wandered across to look at them and assess the amount of work that would need to be done. Most of them seemed to be in fairly good order. The roofs and walls of all of them were sound, although the wooden doors on some were rotten. She looked into some of the darkest corners and wondered if they were ever used by bats. She made a mental note to ring the Bat Conservation Society before making any alterations.

Using a large sketchbook she began to map out how it might look if they were refurbished so that they could be used. She thought that if she could produce a compelling proposal she might be able to get funding from the bank or a charity that helped to preserve old buildings. Even with the short-term lease, a good return could make it a worthwhile investment.

As she sketched, she saw Darwin the cat slip round the back of the stable block and saw what looked like a path running around to the back of the building. She wondered if it led anywhere, or whether it had just been trampled down by the cat.

She completed her plan, adding some colour with broad strokes of marker pen and got up to follow the cat. She

71

brushed the seat of her shorts and slipped her feet back into her sandals, leaving the sketchbook on the chair she had been using.. As she peered around the side of the last stable, she saw that what she had thought was a single row stables was in fact a double row of back-to-back stalls. The row she had already seen faced onto the coach yard, but there was another row behind, facing down the hill, each with a wonderful view of the surrounding countryside. As she watched, she saw Darwin's tail disappearing into the third one along. She followed, and pushed open the door of the stable, calling to the cat, and peering into the darkness.

She had taken off her sunglasses, but the space still seemed to be surprisingly dark, with very little light coming through what she had thought were broken shutters. Moving to the back wall, she banged her shin against something hard and rubbed it before moving on. The shutters pulled back easily on well-oiled hinges, and as she turned back to the room she gasped.

The room was being used as a studio by a sculptor working in copper and steel. The walls were covered in sketches of animals, and the benches were teeming with copper animals of all sizes.

She picked up some of them, marvelling at the way the artist had represented the shape with a few cleverly-chosen strokes, catching the spirit of the animal without being too tediously representational.

She spotted Darwin hiding up in a corner and went to pick him up. As she did so, the door swung wider and a dark shaped filled the opening. She panicked, seeing that her way out was blocked and clutched the cat more tightly. She must have squeezed harder than she intended, as the cat let out a yowl and leapt from her grasp, running out into the yard

Eleanor tried to follow, but her path was blocked by the outline of a man in the doorway . She decided that attack was the best form of defence.

'What on earth are you doing on my property?' she asked.

'*Your* property?' came the unexpected reply. 'I don't think you know who you're talking to.'

As he spoke, Eleanor realised immediately who it was. Nick Preston. Her heart sank. Why was it that they couldn't have a normal friendly relationship as she did with so many other local people?

'Nick, it's me. Eleanor. What's going on here? Who's been working in this....studio?'

'Don't worry,' he said, avoiding the question, 'It won't be here for long.' She waited for him to expand on the explanation.

'My parents want to move to Australia to live with my sister Kate now that she's starting a family, so we'll all be out of your hair before you know it.' The implication was that the studio belonged to his mother or father.

Eleanor was startled at the news that he would be leaving, and astonished at her reaction to it. Much as she disliked Nick, she had got used to seeing him around and feeling the frisson of excitement each time they met. It would be odd to live here without him in the neighbourhood. She could also see that he had reservations about leaving and might perhaps want to stay in Stourton rather than travel to the other side of the world.

As she thought this through, she started to warm to the man, but his next sentence put a stop to that.

'So as soon as you've finished playing shops and make your way back to the city, we can all move on and things can get back to normal around here,' he said roughly.

Eleanor was so shocked she couldn't speak. How *dare* he! She knew that her friends from London, Justin included, thought she was mad to come down to Kent, but she had begun to think that she was fitting in her quite well and had even started to think that she could make a permanent life for herself in the area. Turning away, she pushed past Nick and ran back into the house.

Lying on her bed she looked up at the low-beamed ceiling and floral wallpaper. Her bed was covered with a vintage patchwork quilt and she had filled the room with bits and pieces from Rosie's shop. Was it really all just playacting? Was she pretending to be something she was not?

She must have fallen asleep, because when she awoke the room was in near-darkness and she could hear Rosie calling to her from downstairs.

'Eleanor! Are you up there?' shouted her friend. 'You shouldn't leave the door open like that, you know.'

Splashing water on her face, Eleanor ran down and hugged her friend. In a flurry of words, she told Rosie about the encounter with Nick that afternoon. Rosie was a great listener and at the end of her outburst, Eleanor felt much better.

'What *is* it with that man?' she asked. 'We always seem to be at cross purposes.'

Rosie grinned at her. 'The course of true love ne'er did run smooth.' She nodded sagely, as she passed Eleanor a fresh cup of tea.

'Don't be ridiculous;' countered Eleanor, 'I don't have the least bit of interest in him as a boyfriend.' She turned away and put her cup down on the floor so that her expression was hidden.

'Really?' pushed Rosie, 'You haven't thought about him at all?'

Eleanor reddened. She had thought about Nick, it was true. On the day of the opening she had thought how handsome he had looked and thought about how it would feel to stand with her hands on his chest looking up into those deep brown eyes. She had thought about how it might feel as his arms went around her and her eyes closed as she lifted her face to his...

'He's rude and arrogant and he hates everything about me,' she said, 'So even if I did like him – which I don't – there wouldn't be any point in thinking about it.'

She fiddled with the buttons on her cardigan for a moment. 'And what did he mean about me being the owner? He talked as if *he* owned it. The real owner's name is Katherine Wilkinson, if I remember correctly.'

74

'No idea,' said Rosie breezily, 'But it shouldn't be too hard to find out. I'll grill Audrey next time I see her.'

They spent the rest of the afternoon talking about the Autumn Food Fair, quibbling about whether to call it a Fair or a Fayre and spending a disproportionate amount of time talking about bunting.

By the time Rosie had left, Eleanor had almost forgotten the incident in the stables, but when she went outside to retrieve her forgotten sketch book she heard noises coming from the the stable block and it all came flooding back.

Shivering in the evening chill, she crossed quickly to the door, intending to start the row all over again. This time she would win, she thought, because this time she would be leading the discussion.

But as she got there something stopped her. An odd feeling came over her as she peeked through the door and saw the Nick at his workbench. His back was to her as he worked, alternately bending over the bench and lifting up the piece he was working on to check the progress. There was something timeless about the sight of a man working with metal and fire. The noise of the furnace meant that he didn't hear her as she gently pushed the door open so that she could watch him. Standing outside the ring of light that surrounded him, and half-hidden by the door she knew that he was unaware of her presence

His figure was outlined against the light as he bent over the bench, soldering wings onto the dragonfly he had created. She could see the muscles in his forearms tighten as he used precision strokes to add the final touches. She could see the concentration on his face, and smiled as he pushed irritably at the lock of hair that always fell over his face.

Lifting the dragonfly to the light, he ran his thumb along the wing, checking the gentle curve he had created. Unconsciously, Eleanor raised her hand to her face as he did so. She had not expected fingers so calloused and blackened to move with such sensitivity. She had not expected to react with such intensity to the sight.

Clutching her sketchbook, she moved away quietly and returned to the house.

Chapter Eleven

With October came the wind. It whipped across the open fields, unbroken by the trees which had now started to lose their summer growth. Wet leaves covered every surface and the days were miserable. The trees which had promised generous harvests of sloes, chestnuts and hazel nuts had been damaged by the severity of the wind, and a great deal of the unripe fruit lay at the sides of the roads.

The nights had started to draw in and Eleanor began to close the gallery early. When she had planned to run the gallery, she hadn't realised just how seasonal a rural business could be. If trade slackened off much more over the winter she might even have to consider opening at the weekends only. She was not happy about the inevitable effect this would have on her income.

When she had opened the gallery she had planned to feature one artist a month. Rosie had been the first artist and during the first week in October Eleanor took down most of the pottery and began to hang a series of bold acrylics by a lady artist who lived in one of the surrounding villages.

The change in colour from serene blues to vibrant reds, yellows and pinks gave the gallery a different atmosphere, lifting Eleanor's mood as she filled the walls with the new work. She went outside and collected pine cones and beech masts, which she piled into wooden bowls with unopened horse chestnuts. She had tried opening the cases and knew that the chestnuts themselves would lose their glossy sheen as soon as they were left open to the air.

She had arranged for the artist to come in and be photographed with the work once it was hung and to give a short interview to Maisie, now dubbed The Good Reporter by Rosie and Eleanor, to distinguish her from the girl who had written her that first ghastly review. She hoped that regularly changing the featured artist and putting on a series of specialist events would help to keep the gallery in the local newspaper and make it part of the local culture.

The photo shoot was a success as the artist happened to be a personal friend of the photographer, and the resulting piece written for the local paper was taken up by the county-wide parent paper. Eleanor was pleased with this small success and celebrated with a fish and chip supper which she shared with Darwin.

***

More customers seemed to be making their way to the gallery, especially now that it was featured on several tourist websites, and Eleanor was happy with the way it was progressing. She hoped that the lull in custom that she had projected could be put down to an error in her calculations.

The week before the Autumn Food Fair (not Fayre, which they had deemed to be too pretentious) was a busy one for Eleanor. She had planned to do a lot of the work herself to keep costs down and had asked Mike to help her by driving a hired van to pick up the market stalls they were using as an alternative to marquees and tables.

The night before he was due to collect Eleanor from the gallery, Mike phoned to say that he had had an accident at work. Someone had dropped a hammer on his toe and broken it. It wasn't a bad injury, but it did stop him from driving.

'I can get someone to collect the stalls and drop the van off at your place, but I'm afraid I can't let you have anyone to drive it back to Folkestone,' he said. 'I can let you have my boy James to load and unload the stalls, but he hasn't got a driving licence. Will you be all right to drive the van yourself?'

He could hear the hesitation in her voice, so he continued, 'It's not that big, so you don't need a special licence. It'll be just like driving a 4x4!'

When Eleanor put the phone down she could have cried. She hated the thought of driving the big van down the tiny country roads and she had never been to Folkestone before so the roads would be unfamiliar.

The next morning, true to his word, Mike's friend Bob dropped off the van with Mike's teenaged son James to help with the heavy lifting.

'Jump up into the driving seat and I'll give you a couple of pointers,' he said. 'Just drive it around the car park for a bit until you get the hang of it.' While he was sitting beside her, Eleanor found it reasonably easy to drive, and felt confident that she could get to Folkestone and back without incident. However, as soon as he had left and they were ready to leave, it was a different story.

Eleanor started the van, almost backed it into a border of chrysanthemums, narrowly missed hitting her own car and slid to a halt. The front wheels jammed as she put them into too tight a lock and then slipped on the gravel as she spun them.

Sitting for a moment with her head on the wheel, wishing she had never decided to have an Autumn Fair, she looked up to see a pair of deep brown eyes watching her. She was mortified that Nick had once again seen her having a crisis. She felt that is was unfair that he never seemed to see her when things were going well.

She slid out of the cab and slammed the door, almost slipping on the wet gravel.

'Not one word,' she said, pointing at him, 'Just don't say a word,' and she ran into the house.

He found her sitting in the gallery flicking through the phone book and stood in the doorway until she noticed him. His quiet strength and sympathy made her at once relax and tense. Her first thought at seeing him was relief that he was there to take charge, but this was quickly followed by irritation at the thought that he believed she was incapable of sorting it out herself.

'I can help,' he said, simply.

'Yes, I'm sure you can,' she replied, wiping away what might have been tear from the corner of her eye. 'But have you considered that I might not *want* your help?'

'You may not *want* it, but I think you might *need* it,' he pointed out. 'Isn't tomorrow the day of the Fair?' He leant against the door jamb, comfortable in his surroundings, and happy to wait as long as it took for her to make her decision. From her point of view, he seemed to be waiting for her to agree with him.

'Yes, it is. But if you think I'm going to sit in that cab with you for 45 minutes there and then another 45 minutes back, you've got another thing coming,' she said petulantly, aware of his closeness as she looked up at him.

'I wasn't suggesting that,' he replied, quietly, 'I was thinking of taking James on my own.'

'Oh,' was all she could think of. Once again she found herself at a loss for words in this man's presence.

'Well, thank you. It's all been paid for. It just needs to be dropped off tomorrow. Thanks.'

She was grateful to him. It was a huge weight off her mind to find someone who was willing to step up and take Mike's place. She just hated the thought that she was now indebted to Nick Preston.

Nick moved the van and helped them to set them up with his usual quiet efficiency and then disappeared. Watching him moving the heavy scaffolding poles with ease, he had reminded her of the hero in an action movie. Not only had he done most of the work himself, but he had managed, at the same time, to keep an eye on James and make sure that he was kept safe while working. The lad was clearly in awe of Nick and followed his every request to the letter.

When the stalls were up, she went to look for him and was told he had gone home. Her first thought on finding that he had left was the hope that he would come back the next day to help take them down and then she felt bad that she was imposing upon his time again. Her relationship with him did seem so full of conundrums.

She spent the evening baking, knowing that the cake stall would be one of the things that would definitely make money, and wanting to keep busy. It was almost midnight when she finally turned off the light and fell into bed.

The next day went off without a hitch. Stall holders turned up on time, plenty of visitors came and sales were high. The market stalls had been a great idea, and were a fantastic refuge for the stallholders against the threatening weather. As it happened, the day stayed dry, but the merry striped awnings added a quirky dimension to the day that set the scene.

Visitors were able to browse through antique books and taste a range of local produce from preserves and chutneys to fresh fruit. There were two bakers showing a selection of local breads, a stall selling Italian delicacies, locally made cheese and even an enterprising lady selling edible snails.

With the local brewery in attendance plus apple juice and ice cream, all produced within a twenty mile radius, the fair catered for all tastes.

One of the favourite stalls for the children was a man who carved pumpkins. He had whole stall of ready-carved fruit and vegetables but the great draw was the fact that he was sitting cross-legged on the floor in front of his table carving faces into apples and pears. There was a crowd around his stall as long as he worked and his partner sold steadily as parents bought gourds and pumpkins ready for Haloween.

She was pleased that people were coming into the gallery as well as visiting the stalls and she even made a couple of sales. She made sure she handed out lots of leaflets to remind people where the gallery was and what it was they sold.

She had moved some of the smaller bits of Rosie's blueware into the room that had originally been the snug and had added a few locally-produced craft items.

Hand-painted plates, silk scarves, wooden toys and some unusual jewellery made from recycled glass had all been displayed tastefully together and the customers seemed to like the fact that there were gift items as well as paintings to see inside. While many of them enjoyed nursing a hot drink against the chilly autumn weather, just as many were pleased to get inside and warm up with a cup of tea or hot chocolate.

Generous jugs of sunflowers added a touch of fun to the afternoon, as visitors were unable to stop themselves from saying 'van Gogh' when they saw them. It was a great talking point.

Rosie and Audrey were once again the mainstays of her refreshment team, and Maisie The Good Reporter came along to write up the event for her newspaper, once again taking time to speak to everyone involved and to get the whole story. She seemed to enjoy herself immensely, tripping from stall to stall, listening to what stall-holders had to say as well as talking to the visitors. She had an openness about her that made people feel at ease and encouraged them to open up to her.

Half-way through the afternoon Eleanor ran upstairs to get her camera and raced down to find Rosie.

'Do you know how to use a digital camera?' she asked, then caught the look on Rosie's face, 'Of course you do. Can you do me a favour?'

She asked Rosie to walk round and take photos of as many people as possible, especially those she knew the names of.

'I want to start a Black Cat Gallery website, and photos of this afternoon will be great,' explained Eleanor. 'People will all want to look at the site to see if their own photo is on it.' She gave Rosie a playful push, 'Get going then, I need to get back to my Meet and Greet Station.'

Rosie took the camera, and after checking that Audrey was coping with the demands for tea a biscuits, walked round and took photos of the guests.

At the end of the Fair, Eleanor asked some of the stallholders to leave her a selection of products on a sale-or-return basis, so now she had a shelf of home-made preserves to add to her stock. The local honey, chutney and jam really emphasised that this was a place that was contributed to by all the community and wasn't just for a select few.

***

Eleanor awoke the next day to the clanging sound of metal bars being loaded onto a van. Nick and Jimmy had come over early and were taking down all the stalls. She threw on a dressing gown, ran out and stopped them as they about to drive off, ready to drop off the stalls and the hired van at the same time.

'Hang on a minute. How are you going to get back?' she asked them

'Train,' Nick replied succinctly.

'On a Sunday?' she asked, 'You'll have to wait ages. Just wait for me to get dressed and I'll follow you down in my car and bring you back.'

Nick started to protest, but she had already gone back into the house to change. She quickly washed and dressed, choosing her oldest jeans and jumper so she could help unload the van. In ten minutes, she was ready to go, and the tiny convoy started.

Driving behind the van wasn't easy, as she couldn't always see the road in front of her, but Eleanor was glad that she had offered to do this. The countryside was lovely at this time of year with the hips and haws showing red in the hedgerows. Once they got onto the motorway, she had to hold herself back from putting her foot down as she usually did. She stayed dutifully behind the van, anxious not to lose sight of them.

They dropped off the market stalls without a hitch and returned the van to the hire depot.

'Okay, get in,' she said, indicating her car.

James jumped into the back and Nick slid into the front seat with his normal fluidity.

'This is great!' James enthused. 'How fast does it go?'

'Up to the speed limit and no further,' replied Eleanor with a knowing look. She smiled at Nick, expecting him to join in the joke, but he turned his head to look out of the window.

They set off along the motorway, with Nick watching the scenery go by and never glancing at Eleanor. At they started off, she had brushed her hand against his knee as she changed gear, sending an electric thrill across her hand, but once the car was in DRIVE there was no further awkwardness.

Coming off the motorway, they passed a sign for a McDonalds. James asked if they could stop at the drive-thru. He'd been earning money labouring for his Dad, and offered to treat them. Eleanor was happy to treat him, so she pulled off the road, saying that the least she could do as a thank-you to them was to pay for the meal. As they circled the building, they saw signs informing them that the drive-thru was closed for the day and inviting them to eat inside, with the offer of free fries for their trouble.

Eleanor didn't want to stop while Nick was in the car, but James had already said 'Great, free chips!' and pointed out a parking space. In his enthusiasm, he sounded like a boy half his age and it seemed churlish to disappoint him.

They walked into the restaurant, ordered and sat down. The adults ate in silence, while James provided them with a string of interesting facts about fast food. Eleanor had ordered breakfast and coffee, as this was her first meal of the day, but it seemed that Nick had been up for hours. He settled for a burger and fries. Eleanor was interested to note that her two companions ate their meals in the same way, taking alternate bites of burger and fries, and she was glad to see this boyish side to Nick.

They had almost finished when a young waitress approached them, her hair pulled back from her face in a fashionable undone bun.

'I see this one's too old for parties,' she said, indicating James, 'but do you have any other children?'

Nick and Eleanor looked at one another. Eleanor was embarrassed, but Nick looked mildly amused, 'No, w haven't.'

'Because we do have some great deals on children's parties,' the girl continued, 'Let me leave you some leaflets.'

James thought it was hilarious 'Just wait till I tell my Dad!' but Nick and Eleanor were less than pleased. It just seemed to highlight the problems they were having in maintaining even a normally civil relationship, let alone a romance.

They got back into the car, and the remainder of the journey passed in silence. James plugged in his earphones and pulled up the hood of his sweatshirt , drifting off into a world of his own, and Eleanor and Nick sat in stony silence, each seemingly concentrating on the road ahead. Eleanor dropped James off first, and then drove Nick back to Stourton Hall Farm. She both hated and loved having him in the car. On the one hand she just wanted to drop him off as fast as possible to avoid any further unpleasantness, and on the other hand she wanted to feel his hand on her knee, telling her to stop the car. She wanted to pull into a layby and fall into his arms, feeling his lips on hers. They soon arrived at the farm and he got out of the car.

'Thanks,' he said, 'and he's right – it is a nice car.' He patted the roof, 'Not sure it's the right one for a country girl, though,' and with that passing shot, he strolled off.

As she drove back to her own home, Eleanor thought about what he had said. The car was her pride and joy, but had been bought when she lived in London and really didn't suit her lifestyle down here. She should really sell it and get an estate car or a small van.

She also wondered what he had meant by her being a country girl. He had always seemed to think she was a town girl. Had it been a joke, or was he beginning to think of her as a permanent fixture?

Another thing she wanted to keep in mind was the need to get her website going. She would need to find someone who could do a good job on a small budget. Perhaps someone just setting up in business? She started to think about what she wanted the site to look like and what she would put on it. She only wanted a simple site, giving directions to the gallery and showing some examples of the work of the featured artists. As she thought about it, she thought the she might also be able to offer online sales of the local produce, and possibly prints of the paintings she had in the gallery.

When she got home, Eleanor opened the front door of the gallery to invite visitors, and walked through to the back room. Opening up her laptop, she researched the websites of similar galleries and jotted down some ideas in her notebook.

She picked up her phone, she dialled her old home phone number.

'Hi, Elspeth, it's Eleanor.' She had remembered that Elspeth's brother was a web designer and she asked Elspeth to pass on the email address of The Black Cat Gallery if he would be interested in doing a website for it.

By bedtime, she felt that she had taken a huge step forwards. Despite all the set-backs and the fact that Nick Preston was a constant thorn in her side, she was beginning to think that she might actually be able to make a profit out of running the gallery. All she needed were a few more months and a bit of luck.

Chapter Twelve

The Autumn Food Fair generated a flutter of enthusiasm amongst the locals, and Eleanor was so busy over the next few weeks that she hardly had time to speak to any of her friends. She would occasionally text one or two of them, but she rarely had time for the long phone calls she used to make.

Driving around Stourton to put up posters for the Autumn Fair, she had become acquainted with a lot more people. She always made sure she popped into Rosie's shop when she was in Stourton and started to make friends with the staff in the library, the Post Office and many of the local shops, including the friendly staff at The Kings Head, where she had first stayed.

As October mellowed into November her posters became eclipsed by a riot of advertising for the local Firework Spectacular. This was held annually at Stourton Hall Farm. The farm had two fields conveniently next to each other, one suitable for the fireworks and one for the car park, and the owners, Nick's parents, were generous enough to let the Fireworks Committee use the fields for free as long as they had a say on which charity benefitted from the proceeds.

'Another committee?' Eleanor laughed when she heard about it. She was in Stourton to pick up a few groceries and had dropped in to see Rosie at her shop. 'This town seems to have a committee for everything!'

'Don't knock it,' said Rosie, who was sharing the joke with her, 'It's the only way things get done around here. Things only happen because of the amount of volunteer labour that's used. If we waited for the council to do things nothing would ever happen!'

Eleanor picked up a leaflet, read the details, and then put it back down again. There was no way she was going to an event that was being held at at Nick's home.

'You'd better keep that,' her friend advised, 'so you don't forget what time it starts. In fact, could you take a handful and put them in the gallery?'

'You sound like you're on the committee yourself,' teased Eleanor. 'You're not, are you?'

'As a matter of fact,' replied Rosie, shuffling some papers, 'I am. It's a real seal of approval from the local residents to be allowed to sit on one of the committees. It's a bit like being in the Mason's. It means I'm one of the locals now. I've lived here fourteen years, and this is the first year I've been allowed to join.'

'Well in that case, Madame Committee Member, I'd be glad to take some of your leaflets to put in the gallery,' and she stuffed a big handful into her bag.

'And you'll be coming on the night, won't you?' pushed Rosie.

'It might be nice to have an evening out,' mused Eleanor, pushing back her reservations about it being at Nick's home. Considering the number of people that would be there, the chances of actually running into him would be small, 'Shall we go together?'

'Sorry,' came the apology, 'as a fully-paid-up member of the committee I'm going to have to be there early setting up and manning the door. You'll have to meet me there.'

On her way home, Eleanor had an idea. She had been thinking about her friends from London a lot recently, as the evenings had become cold and the weather was turning. She was feeling guilty about the way that she and Justin has parted on such bad terms and had they had started exchanging a few tentative texts with him in the last week or two.

On impulse, she rang Justin and asked him to bring William and Lucy with him to watch the fireworks. She had plenty of spare rooms now that the house was fully refurbished and they could stay with her. It would be nice to have guests.

November 5th fell on a Saturday and her friends drove down in the afternoon. She had told them the gallery would be open until 5pm and that she would have to work until then, but at a little after 3pm she heard the throb of a 3lt engine as Justin pulled into her drive.

Wrapped up as if they were going on an arctic expedition, her friends squeezed out of the car and ran into the house. Lucy had changed her hair colour again, but the boys looked much as they had before. It seemed that nothing much changed in their world.

'My God, Eleanor, this is *amazing*!' enthused William, looking at the gallery foyer, 'Did you really do all this yourself?'

'Look at all this cute stuff !' called Lucy, rummaging around in the craft room and leaving things lying in disarray. Eleanor walked behind her, replacing things in their proper places.

Justin stood in the doorway looking smug. His carefully-chosen clothes were a little too clean to be the clothes of a country gentleman, which seemed to be the look he was aiming for.

'Couldn't live without me, then?' he smirked. 'Come and give me a kiss.'

Eleanor backed away from him, sitting down smartly in an easy chair as it came in contact with the back of her legs.

'That's not the reason I invited you. I told you that on the phone.' She was beginning to wish that she hadn't invited them at all, now. 'I just didn't want us to part on bad terms. I did make it clear that this was going to be a purely platonic weekend, didn't I?'

'Yes, but you must have known I wouldn't take any notice of that,' said Justin with his normal irritating arrogance. As he walked across and tried to put his arms around her she wondered how she had ever found his attitude attractive. As he hugged her, Audrey walked into the gallery.

'Oh, I say,' she said as she spotted the two in an embrace, 'Do you want me to leave?' Her good breeding meant that there was no way she would intrude upon a private moment uninvited.

'Not in the least,' said Eleanor, relieved, 'Do come in, Audrey. Is there something I can help you with?'

'Yes, dear, I've lost Darwin again. Have you seen him?'

The three friends from London were wandering along the gallery looking at the pictures. They stopped at every other piece to make derogatory remarks, laughing crudely as they did so.

Audrey fixed them with her piercing stare as they made comments about the work of one of her friends. 'Are these people annoying you?' she asked.

'No, it's all right, thanks,' said Eleanor, looking around for the cat, 'They're actually friends of mine.' She turned to call down the gallery, 'Shut up for a moment, you lot, you're embarrassing me.' She rolled her eyes at Audrey and smiled, indicating that they were just joking, and led her in the other direction.

'He's not in here. Do you want to look in the kitchen, while I check the bedroom? He does like it on my quilt.'

Audrey looked unconvinced, but soon found her cat, bundled him into the basket she had brought with her and left. Eleanor knew that she would have to go over the incident when they next met and somehow convince Audrey that they were not being as rude as they seemed.

As soon as she had gone, Lucy and William minced up the gallery arm in arm.

'I say, old girl,' lisped William, 'Have you seen my pussy?'

Everyone except Eleanor laughed, and Lucy joined in the joke, throwing her scarf over her shoulder as if it were a stole.

'I'm sure I left it around here somewhere. It's just that I was distracted by all this dreadful tat and I lost track of when I last saw it.'

'Lucy!' exclaimed Eleanor, 'Don't be so rude!'

'Yes, Lucy,' chimed in Justin, 'Don't be so mean about Eleanor's new friends. I'm sure they have lovely times together. Going on hikes and picnics and such like in the good old country-side.'

'I don't understand you lot,' complained Eleanor. 'I asked you down here to have a lovely evening watching fireworks and catching up on old times and you're just spoiling it. I've started the fire in the drawing room and I thought we could eat in there before we go over to the farm.'

She shut the front door and turned off the lights in the gallery.

'Oh, let's not go to the silly old fireworks,' said Lucy, after they had taken their off boots and settled down with a hot drink, 'Let's just stay here and get blotto in front of the fire like the lords of the manor.'

Eleanor protested that they had to go now that they had agreed to. She had spent a lot of time and effort to make sure that the weekend was a success and was annoyed that it was beginning to go wrong already.

'Is it the £3 a ticket you're worried about losing?' asked Justin, condescendingly, 'I can reimburse you that if you're short of money. Here's a twenty – you can keep the change.' He put the money on the mantelpiece and placed a small brass sculpture on top to keep it from blowing away.

'Of course it's not the money! I promised I would go and I've told everyone I'll be bringing friends with me. We have to go along and show our faces at least.'

William stepped in at this point and calmed everyone down. He suggested that they had dinner and then talked about it afterwards. Eleanor went to the kitchen to heat up the casserole she had prepared, while the others made themselves at home. When she got back they had finished the wine they had brought with them and opened the one she had left out to drink with the meal.

The meal was a merry one, and everyone seemed to forget their differences. Eleanor joined in the fun as they remembered some of the good times they had had together. They had been double-dating for just over two years and they all knew each other well. Sometimes it was as if they were all one big family, with the normal squabbles that families have. At other times, she was unable to think why it was that they had become friends. The things they talked about seemed so shallow to her now.

As the evening drew on, Eleanor looked at the clock and saw that it was approaching 7.30pm.

'Come on, we'd better get going if we're going to catch the fireworks.'

'Don't be silly,' laughed Justin, 'We're not going out now. We're nicely settled in here and I for one am not going out into the countryside at this time of night. Have you seen how dark it is out there?'

Eleanor was livid. 'You never had any intention of going to the fireworks, did you?' she accused him.

'Now hang on a tick,' Justin turned towards her, 'We've come all this way into the middle of nowhere just to see you, and I think that as we are the guests, *we* are the ones who get to say whether we go or not.' He looked smugly at Eleanor, believing that he had won the argument.

'Well everyone will be very disappointed not to meet you,' countered Eleanor, 'I really wanted to go and it will be lovely to come back into the warm and sit by the blazing fire after we've been out in the cold night air.'

Justin seemed to read more into this than she intended. If she realised that he was thinking about the two of them snuggled up together on the rug in front of the fire, she didn't let it show. 'Oh, damn it. Let's go, then. You never know, it might even be a laugh.'

He picked up the keys to his car. 'We'll have to go in my car because I don't think we'll all fit in yours.'

Eleanor's explanation that the farm was just down the lane and that they would be better off walking didn't go down well, although they gave in when she told them that the 'car park' was just a field. They bundled up into their coats and boots and ventured outside.

The cocktail of unlit roads and too much red wine spiced with the biting chill of the November air put William and Lucy in a bad mood. Justin was trying to remain up-beat, buoyed along by his thoughts of what might happen later that night.

Lucy clung to William as they walked along, feigning fright at every rustle in the hedgerows and every hoot of an owl. By the time they arrived at Stourton Hall Farm, Eleanor was beginning to get exasperated with her constant whining.

The Firework Committee had built and lit a huge bonfire in the middle of the field and set up the fireworks to one side, flanked by a loud-speaker system for the accompanying music. The field was full almost to capacity and Eleanor was constantly stopped by people wanting to say hello and to let her know how great the Black Cat Gallery was.

She was proud to show off her new life to her friends, hoping that they would be pleased that she had made such a success of her new life, but they had a scathing remark to make about almost everyone they met. They also passed comment on the way the event had been organised, the setting and the weather.

Eleanor had to keep asking them to keep their voices down as they pointed out the shortcomings of the evening.

At one stage, Justin almost got into a fight with a local farmer when he made a particularly rude comment, but was saved from this by the start of the fireworks.

Even during the fireworks themselves, when everyone else was ooh-ing and aah-ing, William, Justin and Lucy repeatedly made loud comments about the poor quality of the display. By the end, Eleanor couldn't wait to leave.

As the fireworks came to an end, and the crowd turned to leave an announcement was made over the loud speaker to ask everyone to hold back and let the older people leave first. The local Old People's Home had brought the residents out for the evening and they wanted to get them safely back to their transport without being jostled by the crowd. The announcer said that they would be entertained with some popular music as they waited.

'Bugger that,' said Justin, 'I'm getting out of here as fast as I can,' and he started to make his way towards the exit.

'No,' Eleanor called, 'Just wait here for five minutes and they'll tell us when it's OK to go.'

Her friends, however, had started to push their way through the crowds. As they approached the exit she could see that a handful of volunteers were helping the Home's residents along a temporary wooden walkway.

Justin tried to step over the walkway and tripped up as he did so. 'This is bloody dangerous!' he swore as he rubbed his ankle. Taking aim, he kicked the edge of the board, putting it out of alignment with the others.

Eleanor watched as a tall figure turned round from helping a gentleman with a walker to see what had happened. He calmly asked Justin to put the board back into place.

The night was dark and the figure was only dimly outlined against the embers of the dying fire. It could have been any one of the helpers, but it was with a sinking feeling in her heart that Eleanor realised it was Nick. She held her breath as she waited to see what would happen next.

'Oh, get out of the way, Farmer Giles,' Justin's temper was fuelled by the wine from earlier. 'We want to leave and you can't stop us. Come on, you lot.'

As he stepped forward, he aimed a half-hearted punch at Nick and the world seemed to slow down. Everyone had turned to look at what was about to unfold and a hush fell over the crowd. With calm precision, Nick's arm rose and his hand clamped around Justin's wrist. They stood for a moment, frozen in a bizarre tableau until Nick gave Justin an almost imperceptible push. It was only a gently nudge, but it was enough to send Justin sprawling backwards into the mud. The crowd laughed and some people began to clap.

Eleanor was horrified. Her friends had embarrassed her more than she had thought possible during the evening, but now she was truly mortified.

Lucy ran to help Justin up, and was beginning to cry. She slipped in the mud as he pulled against her.

'I don't like it here. I don't like the mud and I don't like the cold and I don't like these horrible people. William, we have to go home'

Justin struggled up and the crowd parted as they walked out of the field. Eleanor could do nothing but follow, wishing she was a million miles away. She kept her head down, but as she passed Nick, she briefly raised her eyes. She could see the disappointment on his face as he recognised her and even in the dark, her cheeks burned. Despite her recent hopes, a relationship with this man was now completely out of the question.

Chapter Thirteen

After the disastrous events of the Firework Spectacular, sales at The Black Cat Gallery began to dwindle. Eleanor tried to put this down to the time of year, but she knew in her heart that the locals had withdrawn the hard-won support that she had been so glad to finally merit. News gets round fast in a small community

The weather seemed to echo her thoughts, and as the garden plants withered and died, so did her hopes for the future.

The only bright spot in her life was the fact that she had seen a family of hedgehogs become regular visitors throughout the autumn, and she now believed they had hibernated underneath an old wood pile left by the previous tenants. She liked to think of the curled up together, warm and secure, just riding it out until the spring.

William, Lucy and Justin had returned home after the Fireworks and apart from one brief text from Lucy, she hadn't heard from them again.

On some of the darker afternoons, when rain threatened and the temperature plummeted she thought about her former life. Had she acted in that way when she had living in London? She was sad to admit that she might well have done on some occasions.

She had fought so hard to win a place in the hearts of the local community and one horrible evening seemed to have not only destroyed any good will she had built up, but also to have built new obstacles to her success. The event had made the local paper, and she had been named as the person who had invited these ill-mannered interlopers.

Hoping to kick-start the business again, she arranged a Christmas Fair, choosing a range of local goods to display in a festive manner, but stopping short of arranging outside stallholders to come along. She booked carol singers and hired metres of fairy lights to go around the garden. From inside the gallery, as well as from the car park, it all looked very inviting.

She spent a lot of time ringing round every contact she had inviting people to event, but a lot of them seemed to be suddenly very busy. She advertised as much as she could in the local paper and by putting up posters and pulled out all the stops to put on a good show, decorating the whole house in her enthusiasm.

The garden proved to be a great source of inspiration, and Eleanor was able to find both holly and ivy to decorate the gallery. She even saw a robin in the garden, but doubted many people would stay outside long enough to see it. She hoped that they would all run inside to the gallery and be so bowled over by what they saw they would take the opportunity to stock upon Christmas presents.

Chopping fruit for the mulled wine, Eleanor found that she was sharing her thoughts with the cat, and realised that she was actually very lonely.

Her days were full to capacity, but she missed the opportunity to share her thoughts with someone close to her. Someone who really knew her well and would not judge her if she said something stupid or unreasonable. Someone with whom she was not afraid to be herself.

     ***

Despite a disproportionate amount of advertising and the offer of free mulled wine and mince pies, very few people turned up on the day of the Christmas Fair. Those who did had come from outside of the local area. It seemed that the local people had well and truly turned their backs on her.

One of the local people who did come along was Audrey, who had become a firm friend to Eleanor. Despite the difference in age, their love of the cat, Darwin, had drawn them together, and the fact that they were both single helped them to bond. They were kindred spirits.

They opened the doors at 10am and waited for the first visitors to arrive. By lunchtime, only fifteen people had visited, and they were beginning to get downhearted.

After a miserable hour and a half over the lunch period when there were no visitors at all, things began to change. The carol singers arrived, bringing with them a welcome wave of gaiety. Mulled wine circulated and the atmosphere improved. During the afternoon, a steady flow of visitors kept them busy, but they made no large sales, with most people opting to buy gifts from the craft section or greetings cards. The carol singers lefts at 4pm and with the light fading outside, they closed the doors.

Walking through to the kitchen, Eleanor and Audrey picked over what went wrong and cleared away the glasses and plates from the refreshments.

'What shall I do with all this mulled wine?' Eleanor asked her friend.

'I think you'll have to throw it away. It seems a shame, but I don't think it will keep.' The two ladies stood and stared into the bowl for a moment, then laughed.

'Look at us! We must look like two of the witches from Macbeth stirring a cauldron!' said Eleanor. 'Let's have one last glass and then the rest of it will have to go on the compost heap.'

'Just one more, then,' agreed Audrey, ' and then I must be going, I need to feed Darwin, and then I'm supposed to be going to Carol Singing practice.' She sighed, 'I might just give it a miss tonight. After all these years, I do know the words quite well!'

The friends drank their wine and chatted about the few sales they had made at the fair.

'Perhaps the winter just isn't a good time for selling art,' mused Eleanor. 'I'll have to think about some other ways of getting people to come to the gallery. This is turning out to be a harder job than I imagined.'

When they had finished their wine, Eleanor offered Audrey another glass, but she declined.

'No, I really must be going this time. I'll see you next Wednesday.' She pecked Eleanor on the cheek and gave her a quick hug. 'And don't give yourself a heart attack worrying about the gallery. I'm sure it will all come right in the end.'

The weather had turned, but despite the cold, there was no likelihood of a white Christmas. Eleanor was quite disappointed and had been looking forward to seeing the countryside covered in a blanket of snow. Somehow it seemed quite comforting to think about snuggling up indoors wrapped in a quilt looking out at a scene that could have come from a Victorian Christmas card.

As the Christmas break loomed on the horizon she found that she needed to make a decision about where to spend the holiday. Her parents were going to Scotland and had invited her to meet them there. Alternatively, she could go back to London; she had also had an invitation from Elspeth, who had rented her flat, to go with her on a skiing holiday, although she reluctantly decided that it was out of the question due to the cost.

In the end, she told them all that she had to stay at the gallery because she had work to do. Feeling sorry for herself, she planned to stay on her own with Darwin, if he deigned to turn up, or on her own if he preferred to stay away.

The frosty mornings were all that she could have hoped for. The delicate fronds of the plants in her garden were covered in a thousand crystals and the sugar-coated branches of the bushes rustled as she passed. Wrapping up warmly, she would often wander through the country lanes early in the morning, catching sight of partridges or rabbits in the fields, and seeing their footprints in the snow.

She put up a bird table outside her kitchen window which she kept stocked with a variety of foods. She remembered how she had looked at the birds when she had first arrived and not known their names. She now knew their names, recognised their songs and knew which ones liked to eat which snacks. She loved the cheeky robins, even though they bullied some of the other birds, and looked out for the pretty thrushes early in the morning.

She now kept the gallery open seven days a week, so that she had an excuse not to go into Stourton. She had her groceries delivered by the local supermarket and sat by the fire in the evening watching the television or downloading films. She knew that she couldn't go on like this and on some evenings, when she was feeling particularly low, she thought about leaving the area altogether.

Occasionally, when she looked out of the back window she would see Nick's car parked by the stable block and catch the dim glow of light from his studio. This told her that he was out there again, working on his sculptures. She longed to walk over there, apologise and be immediately forgiven. She imagined being wrapped in those strong arms as he stroked her hair and told her everything would be all right. On these the occasions that she locked the door tight and turned up the volume on her MP3 player, strengthening her resolve not to go begging.

She had lived here for six months now and at this moment she felt completely alone. Apart from Rosie, she had made no really close friends locally, and she had pretty much broken off relations with her friends from London. How good it would be to find someone she could share her life with. She imagined that Nick would make a great partner, strong and capable and caring. She imagined what it would be like to live in this house with him and wondered what he would think of the way she had decorated it. It was all foolish fantasy, she knew, as the house was due to be knocked down and by this time next year, fourteen brand new houses would stand on this site.

At this point in her thoughts, her memories of the Firework night fiasco always brought her back to reality. She couldn't even look at Nick now, let alone speak to him, and he had always shown so much disdain of her as a city girl, that he must now have had his thoughts confirmed.

***

One frosty evening, Rosie came to call unexpectedly. Opening the front door, Eleanor saw her friend's breath on the cold night air and knew that the night would be a cold one. She ushered Rosie in, and closed the door to keep out the cold night air.

'Let me take your coat,' she said, holding out her hands, 'Is that anther new hat?'

Rosie was very fond of hats and the one she wore today was knitted in a rainbow of colours. Pulled down low over her ears, it made the escaping wisps of hair looked as if they had a life of their own.

'You can never have too many hats,' she told Eleanor.

'Hi, Darwin!' she threw herself down on the settee, and pulled the cat on to her lap, 'Long time no see. How's it going?'

Eleanor sighed, replying for the cat 'After Fireworks night, how do you think?' She held up the kettle, offering tea, and Rosie nodded.

'Oh, don't mind about that, the new gossip is all about the by-pass. I don't think anybody even remembers Fireworks Night.' Eleanor was comforted by this, but not totally convinced that Rosie was telling the truth. She was happy that her friend cared enough to lie, but she knew how long a country memory could be.

They chatted about their families, their respective businesses and about whether it was likely to be a white Christmas, and then Rosie brought up the question of going to church.

'I'm not really a church-goer,' admitted Eleanor, 'So I think I'll have to say 'no' to this one. Even if it is Christmas.'

'How about coming to Christingle then?' asked Rosie, tucking her hair behind her ears, 'It'll be lovely with all the children there and the crib will be out. It's a great local tradition and it's so pretty.'

Eleanor still wasn't convinced that she wanted to go, so Rosie changed tack and invited her instead to come down to the local pub that Saturday, when the Hoodeners were playing .

'What's that, then?' asked Eleanor

'It's a bit like a cross between Morris Dancing and a Mummers play,' replied Rosie.

'Really? They still do that?'

'Well, I don't know about 'they', but we still have it round here. The group dress up and perform a play, sing some rowdy songs and everyone stumps up a pound or two for charity. It's all a bit silly, but great fun.'

Eleanor agreed to let Rosie and Daniel pick her up after dinner the following Saturday and she found that she was looking forward to the evening. It was such a long time since she'd been out, that it would make a nice change.

She wrapped up warmly for the evening, not knowing how long they would be standing outside for. As she dressed, she looked in the mirror and saw that she had become thinner since she had lived in Kent. Her hair had grown longer, and she noticed that it had started to curl at the ends. This is something she would never have put up with in London; the straighteners would have been out in a flash if she had noticed it happening. She smoothed down the curls, knowing that there were many more important things in her life than her hairstyle.

She noticed that her wardrobe had changed, too. Gone were the fitted dresses and court shoes. Instead she now had jeans for every day of the week and three pairs of wellies – one pair in the front porch, one in the back and a pair in the car in case she got stuck in the mud.

The Saturday of the Hooded ners outing was cold, but clear and the stars sparkled in the night sky. This was something that Eleanor always noticed about living in Kent. The light pollution didn't mask the stars in the night sky the way it did in the city, and it was possible to follow the planets as they moved across the night sky.

The pub was crowded and Eleanor and Rosie stayed outside while Daniel pushed his way to the bar for drinks.

The Hooded ners weren't due to perform until quite late in the evening, and a folk band was playing softly as they arrived.

The landlord had decorated the bar and garden in traditional fashion, with lots of holly and ivy on top of the obligatory rows of hop vines. The garlands were wrapped with rows of fairy lights turned to the 'twinkle' setting, which gave the whole thing a magical effect. Everyone around was friendly, and there seemed to be a sense of anticipation in the people who gathered there. They all spoke in hushed tones, waiting for something to happen.

Rosie and Eleanor found a seat and settled in for the performance, listening to the gentle tones of the folk band as they performed a repertoire of traditional folk tunes. The voice of the lead singer was sweet and travelled in the cold night air, caught by the wind and that whisked it away forever across the downs.

As Daniel came out with their drinks, Eleanor noticed a familiar figure following him. Nick, however, was with friends and she didn't think he'd seen her. Her involuntary thought that she was glad she had put on some make-up seemed unnecessary.

Instead of being pleased to see Nick, she found that his being there spoilt the evening for her, and she spent a lot of time looking around to see where he had gone. When she lost sight of him she was worried in case he appeared suddenly behind her, and when she could see him, she felt torn between wanting to leave and wanting to walk over to be with him.

The Hoodening was a spectacular success, and everyone seemed to enjoy it, cheering the hero on, boo-ing the bad guy and laughing at the fool. As they watched, Eleanor realised that this same play had been performed outside this same pub for hundreds of years. It humbled her to think that she was now part of this local tradition.

She noticed several people in the audience that she knew, and who had greeted her with enthusiasm in the early part of the Fireworks Night, but nobody took the time to say hello to her this time. She felt snubbed, and when Daniel and Rosie dropped her off at home, she felt as if the evening had not been an unqualified success.

Despite this and the confusion she felt at seeing Nick, and the chance that she might see him again, she agreed to join Rosie and Daniel to watch the Carol Singers in Market

Square on Christmas Eve. They were so kind to her that she was loath to let them down.

With the promise of snow, and the scent of mulled cider in the air, the Market Square was as festive as it could be. The Rotary Club had put up a few stalls, beautifully decorated with yards of tinsel in all colours, and the Sea Cadets' band was going to play and lead the singing. It was a real community event.

The three friends found a spot near the front and perched on the edge of a low wall to listen. Eleanor had her hands thrust in her pockets against the cold, and was well muffled in her woolly hat and scarf. She had tucked the money she was going to put in the collection tin into the palm of her hand inside her glove, and the feel of it made her think about the journeys to school in the winter months with her dinner money held safely inside her mittens.

As she stood in the crowd, Eleanor felt someone push past her and moved slightly forward, thinking that someone wanted to get past.

'Sorry,' came the apology. She stiffened, a turned her head slightly, not knowing what to say. Nick was standing awkwardly behind her, holding out a plate of mince pies. 'Mince pie?' The expression on his face was unclear, but the pie was unmistakeably a peace offering. He looked as if he were about to say something but no words came out.

Stunned, Eleanor took a pie and started to eat it, even though her throat had suddenly turned dry. With her mouth full, she couldn't speak and she tried to signal her thanks with her eyes. By the time she had finished eating, he had vanished again and she groaned inwardly when she thought about what she must have looked like.

Rosie laughed, brushing crumbs from her mouth, 'Well, that was odd. Nice mince pies, though.'

Daniel had his arm around his wife, and Eleanor envied their close relationship. Their happiness only served to highlight her own loneliness. Although she looked for him, Nick was nowhere to be seen for the rest of the evening.

She mulled over what the offer of a mince pie had meant. It had obviously been meant as a peace offering and as she had taken one, she had signalled that she was ready to be friends, but was that all? Did he want more? She was beginning to think that *she* did. By the end of the evening she was more confused than ever and went straight to bed when she got home.

***

On Christmas morning, she opened the presents her parents had sent down to her and put on the television. Old films were just what she needed, she thought, so she staying in her pyjamas and threw some more logs on the fire.

As the day wore on, the fire grew low and she needed to go outside to fetch more wood. Throwing on a coat, she discarded her slippers and pulled on her wellington boots.

It wasn't until she had an armful of wood and was half-way across the yard that she heard the sound from Nick's workshop. She hurried back towards the kitchen door, but as she did so, the tapping sound stopped and she saw Nick coming around the side of the building.

She had never felt more of a fool than she did at that moment. Standing in the middle of the yard in a puddle of slushy snow that had never properly settled, wearing brushed cotton teddy pyjamas, a duffle coat and wellies. She had brushed her teeth, but done nothing with her hair, which she now imagined must be sticking up every which way.

Nick looked surprised to see her, 'I thought you'd gone away for Christmas.'

She turned to face him, 'No, I thought I'd stay here.'

In three easy strides, he crossed the yard and held out his arms. For one moment, she thought he was going to sweep her off her feet and her eyes widened, but he stopped in front of her and put his hands around the wood.

She stammered her thanks and wondered how it was that this man made her feel so foolish each time they met.

She followed him back into the house, and showed him where to put the wood.

As he turned to go, she realised that she had followed too closely, and as he stood up from the log basked he almost knocked into her. Once again, he put out his hands, and this time he did embrace her. He pulled her roughly to him and held her close. She could feel the heart beating inside his chest, and she drank in the smell of him. He pulled back slightly, looking down into at her, his expression unreadable. Cupping her face in his hands, he kissed her gently, for what seemed like an eternity. Then, without warning, he pulled away, apologised and left.

The back door banged on its hinges, bringing in gusts of cold air. Eleanor didn't move, wondering if it had all been a dream. Touching her lips, she knew that it hadn't been, and she wondered what his sudden exit had meant.

Smiling to herself, she decided that the kiss might have been the Christmas present she had been waiting for.

Chapter Fourteen

January was a bad month for sales. As well as the annual belt-tightening, people tended to stay indoors, only going out to buy things they needed or to travel to the local large town or outlet centre for the sales. This January was one of the worst kind. The weather was the wet and windy kind, not the dry, crisp kind, and the whole world began to look unkempt and dirty. Most of the trees and bushes in Eleanor's garden were dormant, with only the dangling catkins of the hazelnut trees showing that spring was on its way.

Eleanor had not seen Nick since Christmas Day and was beginning to think she had dreamt the whole episode.

Being a quiet month for, she decided to take a holiday and she closed the gallery for a week so she could visit her parents in Scotland. It was nice to see them, of course, but she worried about the gallery the whole time she was there and was glad to come home.

The day she returned was a dark, overcast day, and when the taxi dropped her off at the end of her drive, she stopped for a minute to look at the gallery. The front entrance did look welcoming. The lights in the gallery were now on an automatic switch, and due to the low light levels were blazing brightly. She was proud of what she had achieved, but for some reason she hesitated before going inside. She had built up a business from nothing, and was paying her way each month. She loved living in the countryside instead of in the constant noise and bustle of London, and yet she felt there was something missing from her life.

When she opened the door she saw a pile of bills waiting for her on the mat. She called for the cat, but her only answer was the echo of her own voice along the length of the gallery. No flash of brown fur as Darwin pushed past her into the kitchen. She dumped her bags on the floor and picked up the envelopes that lay there.

She was still sorting through the mail when Audrey drove up and asked if she could have a word. Worried, Eleanor took her post through to the kitchen, made her a cup of tea and prepared to listen.

She needn't have worried, as Audrey's only concern was that one of the cats she had rescued was fighting with her other cats. As they talked about the problem the solution became obvious – Eleanor would take the cat and Audrey could visit as often as she liked.

This was just the fillip Eleanor had been waiting for. Audrey brought the cat round the very next day, and it seemed to feel at home in the gallery.

'He doesn't mind Darwin,' said Audrey, 'So it won't be a problem when he comes to call.'

The new cat was tabby and white, and a complete contrast to Darwin. Being so much younger, he wanted Eleanor to play with him a lot of the time, and she soon came to love him as much as she did Darwin.

The days were bright, if cold, and the first snowdrops began to appear. Eleanor wondered if she should learn a bit more about gardening so that she could bring some more colour into the front entrance of the gallery. She flipped open her laptop and found the website of the local garden centre. Seeing that she had missed the right time to plant bulbs for spring colour, she made a resolution to drive over and see if she could buy some ready-planted in pots as soon as she could.

Her cat, Tommy, fitted into her life style very well, as he seemed to sleep for most of the day and wake up in the evening. Very often she would go into the bedroom and find the two cats curled up on the quilt together, so that they look as if they were just one animal. Eleanor was building up a collection of cute cat photos and was beginning to think of them as 'her babies'.

As January melted into February, The Black Cat Gallery once more began to take money. Eleanor continued to change the featured artist each month and was hoping that her Mother's Day Fair would be similar to the successful Autumn Fair.

The day before Pancake Day, she received a phone call from someone in London who had mentioned The Black Cat Gallery to an artist friend she had met. This artist was quite well-known and had been born near Stourton. Eleanor's friend had convinced the artist that it would be a good idea to exhibit in The Black Cat and had passed on the phone number.

Thrilled with the news, Eleanor rang the artist, booked her in for a March exhibition and arranged for her to come to Kent to view the space as soon as possible. Ending the call, Eleanor quickly tapped in Rosie's number to tell her the good news.

Rosie, as always, was supportive and full of enthusiasm for both the coming exhibition and the idea of a Mother's Day Fair. The friends agreed to meet in Stourton for a coffee and a chat.

As they sat in the window of the coffee shop, Rosie told Eleanor a little bit about the history of the area. Eleanor's chair was facing the window and she watched the people go past as her friend talked.

Her heart skipped a beat when she saw Nick turn the corner. She watched as he moved with his usual slow grace up to the window of the greengrocers and stood looking at the display. Her heart warmed as she thought of him doing something as mundane as choosing potatoes and wondered what he would do if she walked up behind him and slid her arms around his waist. Would he turn and kiss her, laughing at the fact that she had startled him?

The next moment, she felt like someone had thrown cold water in her face. A tall, athletic-looking blonde girl came out of the shop, put her arm through Nick's and pulled him down the street. Eleanor could see the affection in his eyes as he looked down at this person. But who was she? They seemed very familiar. It must be his girlfriend, and that must have been the reason he had left so quickly when they had kissed. The guilt of thinking about this girl must have been what had stopped him.

Once again, Eleanor had been made to feel like an idiot. She had thought that a romance could be about to happen, but Nick already had a girlfriend, and this was the reason he had been so distant with her. The couple stopped outside the next shop they came to and Nick went in first. As the blonde girl followed, she put her hand possessively on Nick's lower back and Eleanor caught the glint of a ring on the fourth finger of her left hand.

'Are you all right?' Rosie asked her, stopping in the middle of a sentence, 'You've gone very pale. You're not going to faint are you?'

Finishing her coffee she apologised to Rosie, 'No, I'm fine, I just ... actually, I think I might be coming down with something. I'm sorry, but I think I'll go home now.'

She assured Rosie that she was capable of driving home safely Stumbling to the car she somehow managed to drive back to the gallery without incident. Curling up with the cats she put '*The Notebook*' into the DVD player and comforted herself with a good cry.

'You idiot,' she told herself. 'Pretending you're an independent businesswoman in control of her own life and then crying over a romance that never was.'

Things went from bad to worse in Eleanor's life. The Private View of the artist from London had been a disaster. Very few people had travelled from London and once again, Eleanor felt that the local townspeople were punishing her for bringing her crass friends to the Fireworks. She felt that they still remembered the evening and were tarring her with the same brush. People in the country had very long memories, she thought.

In a fit of self-pity Eleanor decided to cancel the Mother's Day Fair, imaging that it could only be a disaster. She immediately regretted it; she needed the income that an event like this would generate. To compensate, she booked an interview on the local radio station with the DJ who had interviewed her before, hoping for the same favourable response. She decided to advertise that the work was all reduced in price, taking the cut from her own commission, so that the artists were still received a fair price. She hoped that the reduced prices might encourage sales.

She used the time on air to advertise the fact that she was having a sale at the gallery and that all the work would be 10% off. The DJ asked her if it was a closing down sale, and although she denied it, the thought seemed to stick in his mind, as he used the phrase in his closing remarks.

Her phone rang before she had even got home, and Rosie asked her if the rumours were true.

'Jan just told me she heard you on the radio saying that you were closing down. Is that true? Why didn't you tell me?'

Eleanor told her that the DJ had made a mistake and asked Rosie to correct anyone she heard repeating it. This was just one more headache to add to her list of problems.

'Why don't you go to the papers and get them to run a piece about the sale, making sure they say that you're not closing down?'

Agreeing that this was a good idea, Eleanor was about to hang up the phone when she had a thought.

'Rosie, did you know that Nick makes animal sculptures out of copper?'

Rosie thought for a moment and then said 'Nick Preston? I have seen copper sculptures like that in that gallery in Whitstable, but they're by someone called Nick Martin. Are you sure you've got the right person? Give me a moment and I'll text you a photo of Nick Martin's work.'

The gallery was unusually busy for the rest of the day and Eleanor didn't have a chance to check her phone until she closed. When she did, she found that Rosie had texted her a photo. As promised, it was a copper sculpture. This one was a rabbit cleaning its face, looking so real it almost moved. Under it she had written 'yes – Nick MARTIN'.

Eleanor checked the internet and found a gallery that stocked the work. In the morning she would ring up and ask them about this artist. Surely there couldn't be *two* artists called Nick doing such similar work?

'Well, curiouser and curiouser, to coin a phrase,' she mused.

She spent the rest of the day fielding phone calls about the impending closure of the galley and taking down any work that she didn't want to feature in the sale. When the last customer of the day had left, she took her accounts into the kitchen and sat up late in to the night at the kitchen table to finish them.

The next day was again overcast and rain threatened. Audrey came over the see how Tom the cat was getting on. Parking her car, she looked at the view for a while before coming to the front door. It was as if she was looking for something.

'It's a good job you're on a hill up here,' she told Eleanor, 'They're forecasting floods next weekend.'

'Do you often get flooded?'

'No, but when we do, it can get really bad. Especially after all this rain we've been having. The ground is soaked and can't take any more water.' Audrey stroked the cat. 'I'm sure you and I will be fine, but Stourton will suffer if it gets flooded again.'

'Has it been flooded before?' asked Eleanor.

'Oh, yes,' remembered Audrey, 'It used to flood every four or five years until they dredged the river and made it wider. The way it had silted up over the years meant that the water didn't have anywhere to go.'

Eleanor pondered on the impact that this might have on a village like Stourton. 'So when was the last time it happened?'

Audrey sat at the kitchen table, watching the cats play with a feather that had blown in while Eleanor made tea.

'Let me think,' she said, looking around the room, as if she would suddenly find the answer written on the walls, 'It must have been about twenty years ago. How time flies. The whole town was covered in about two foot of water. It doesn't sound much, but believe me, when it's sloshing around in your front room it looks like an awful lot!'

Eleanor poured the tea and offered Audrey a biscuit.

'Was there much damage?' she asked.

'Well, nobody was expecting it, you see. We'd all been told that the water would be carried away by the river and it was a complete shock to everyone. Lots of people didn't have the proper insurance, and half a dozen or so businesses went under. I think they've got pictures in the Local History section at the library if you're interested.'

Eleanor didn't think that she wanted to look at the pictures just to gloat over the misfortune of others, but on the other hand, she was interested in the history of Stourton.

'I might just do that,' she said, 'Was anybody hurt?'

A strange look came over Audrey's face, which Eleanor found it hard to interpret.

'Oh, my dear,' she said, 'That was the year of the Preston tragedy. I don't want to gossip, but seeing as you're quite involved with the family, I think you ought to know.'

Eleanor failed to see why Audrey should think she was more involved with the Preston family than with any other, but chose to ignore the comment. 'Why, what happened?'

Audrey took a sip of tea and placed the cup back on its saucer with her usual precise neatness.

'The three Preston children were out in the fields when the rain started, and their mother couldn't find them. This was before the days when every child carried a mobile phone. Are you sure you want to hear this, dear?'

Eleanor nodded.

'I won't go into all the horrid details, but the three children were down by the river and the little boy fell in. The two older children jumped in to try to save him, but he was swept away and they didn't find the body until the next day.'

The two women looked at each other wordlessly, each thinking of the suffering that this sad accident must have caused the family.

'The two older children weren't to blame, of course – it was just one of those things, but it obviously hit them hard

113

and I think it brought them closer together. They were almost inseparable after that,' Audrey took another sip of tea. 'And now no-one talks about it. I suppose the family still remember the day it happened, but life goes on, people move away, and little Simon is all but forgotten.'

The conversation moved on to a happier topic, and Eleanor salted away this information about Nick for a later time. There was obviously more to him than met the eye.

Chapter Fifteen

'Well, I don't know about April showers,' said Eleanor to Rosie the next day when she visited, 'but we've certainly had a lot of March showers.'

Rosie was wrapped in a chunky-knit cardigan with huge buttons in bright citrus colours. She had chosen a necklace of over-sized wooden beads that matched perfectly.

'That's a nice necklace,' said Eleanor, as soon as she noticed it.

'Thanks, I got it from the charity shop. The person that gave it in was either very generous or had no style. I think it's fab!'

Eleanor ushered her into the gallery and they pulled two chairs closely together so that they could chat and still serve any customers that came in. The front door needed to be kept open, but a heavy Victorian screen diverted the draft and a fan heated warmed their feet.

The phone rang while they were getting settled, and Eleanor answered it while Rosie went through to the kitchen to make tea for them both. Rummaging in the cupboards, she found a packet of biscuits, which she took through with the tea.

'Are you totting up all the money you're making?' she asked, leaning over to see what Eleanor was doing on her laptop.

'It's my accounts spreadsheet, yes, but I'm not making much money.'

The gallery was still only just breaking even, and Eleanor was almost at her wit's end thinking of ways to make it pay. Her initial calculations had not taken into account the fluctuation in the number of seasonal visitors.

Rosie told her that she had visited the gallery showing Nick Martin's work and it seemed that Nick Martin and Nick Preston *were* one and the same person. His full name was Nicholas Martin Preston and he had dropped his surname to create a pseudonym for his artwork. He wanted to preserve his anonymity and keep his carpentry business separate.

'I knew it!' crowed Eleanor triumphantly. 'The sneaky so-and-so!'

'I'm going to go over there and get him to exhibit with me just as soon as I can. It doesn't matter that he has a girlfriend; we're both adults and I'm sure we can work this out.'

Even as she said it, her resolve wavered. She ran her fingernail along the side of the table. 'It's not as if we were even going out or anything,' she pointed out, 'It'll be OK, won't it?' She looked up from the hair that had fallen across her face, and Rosie felt a pang of sympathy for her. Eleanor was trying so hard to find her way in the world, and at the moment everything seemed to be against her. Rosie leant forward and hugged her friend.

'It'll be fine,' she promised.

She hadn't told Rosie about the Christmas kiss, because she had wanted to keep it as her own special secret, but Rosie had guessed that she had feelings for Nick. Looking back, she supposed it was quite obvious, especially to someone as close to her as Rosie.

'Go over there now,' Rosie encouraged, 'I think I heard a noise coming from there earlier.'

'No, I won't go now, I'm in the middle of things here,' said Eleanor, who was patently sitting down having a cup of tea with nothing else to do. 'I'll go later.'

'As long as you promise to go and don't keep putting it off,' her friend warned, 'You really do need this.'

They moved off the topic of Nick and spoke about Rosie's new line of ceramics. She had started to design a range of mugs showing local scenes, and with the names of local places etched into them. She was hoping they might become as popular as the traditional Devon ware that was so collectable. They talked about the age-old artists conundrum of needing to earn money while at the same time not wanting to 'sell out'. By the time it was dark, they were still chatting, and it was time for Rosie to leave.

When Rosie had gone, Eleanor cleared away the tea things, locked up the gallery and then peeped out of the back window and decided that she had to take the bull by the horns and go over there while she still had the courage. She checked her make-up, changed her shirt and after two false starts, walked across the yard.

Nick stopped what he was doing and looked up as she entered. For a long minute they stood like that, each waiting for the other person to say something. Eleanor felt her legs wobble a little as she took a step into the studio. It was hot in the studio with the forge on full, and Nick had unbuttoned his shirt. That one lock of hair still hung forward over his left eye and Eleanor felt a catch in her throat as she thought of Nick's blonde girlfriend moving it tenderly away from his face.

She knew what it felt like to be held in those arms and had to put her hand on the bench to stop herself from moving any further towards him, pushing aside the tools that lay there. The gentle clink of metal spurred her into action. He had a girlfriend, she reminded herself, and she was here as a potential business partner; she didn't want him to think she was mooning over him like a silly school girl.

Her breath came fast as she blurted out, 'I like your work, will you put it in the gallery?'

He seemed surprised at this and blinked, pushing the hair back with one hand. She felt a pang of disappointment that it had moved out of her reach, and took a deep breath.

'Can you put some of your work into the gallery?' she repeated. 'Please?'

He moved towards her.

'Eleanor,' he breathed softly, putting his hand on her arm, and then hesitated. She wondered if he, too, had felt the sting of electricity as he had touched her. In a panic, she pulled away and took a step backwards. He looked confused and took a step towards her, but she moved back even further so that she was standing just outside the gallery, and out of his reach.

'If you don't want to, that's fine,' she continued, determined to say what she had come to say, 'but if you do, just drop it off any time. You know where I am.'

She fled, and didn't stop running until she was upstairs on the bed with the cats pulled close to her. Darwin rebelled and ran downstairs, but Tommy stayed to comfort here.

'I must be the most stupid person of all time,' she told the cat, 'why on earth did I say 'you know where I am'? Never mind, I'll just have to think of another way to keep this gallery afloat.'

The next day she had an appointment with another potential exhibitor and closed the gallery for an hour. With the sales as low as they were, she didn't see that it would matter that much. Putting on her most professional outfit, she dropped her laptop into its case and hurried out of the door, keen to be on time and to present a good impression.

The meeting was a success, and driving back through the country roads she spotted a bank of pale yellow primroses, so different from the brash neon yellow of the primula plants at the garden centre. She was even happier when she had to wait behind a dustbin lorry and spotted some patches of celandine in the depths of the coppiced woodland next to the road. The sight of the unpretentious little flowers reminded her of a Shakespeare play, and she was cheered to think that the same flowers had been growing in that same patch year after year.

When she got back to the gallery, she had the shock of her life. In her absence the space had been transformed. Animals of all shapes and sizes stood, crouched, crawled, flew and lay on every surface. For a moment, she just stood and stared. Then she walked around the gallery, looking at every single piece and touching the most sensitively portrayed ones: a mother duck and her ducklings, a sleeping cat and a tiny mouse hiding under a leaf.

It was hard to see how he had managed it, but the clean lines of the gallery had been hidden and somehow a fluidity of expression had been introduced. Visitors would be drawn through the exhibition from piece to piece by clever placement and visual cues.

Eleanor was speechless. Nick had known exactly which pieces to bring and the best way to display them. He can come across and done this for her, in her absence, as a gift. It was a sign that he was ready to put the past behind them, let bygones be bygones and to move their relationship forward.

She left the gallery and zipped out of the back door and she skipped round to Nick's studio to thank him. She was smiling like a child with a bowl-ful of ice-cream but she stopped dead at the door as if she had run into a wall. Nick stood by the back window with his arm raised as he had been when she had seen him the previous time. His cotton shirt fell down below the waist of his cargo pants, but with one hand raised, a it had lifted to show a tempting flash of toned, and tanned, flesh . In the other hand he held the same dragonfly as before. The difference was that the blonde she had seen him with in Stourton was now standing next to him. Their heads were almost touching as he pointed out the work he had done on the wings.

They turned as one as they head Eleanor approaching, their bodies moving gracefully in synchronisation.

'Eleanor, I don't think you know Kate.' Eleanor found it hard to hear his voice through the ringing sound in her ears. Her head was spinning and she felt as if she had just jumped from a moving merry-go-round.

'How do you do,' she said quickly, 'Well, I can't stay, I just came to say thanks for the stuff. I'll catch you later,' and once again she bolted for home like a frightened rabbit. This really wasn't going well at all.

Over the next week, she seemed to have an unexplained increase in the number of visitors at the gallery and one by one Nick's pieces began to get sold. Some people were even asking if he took commissions, and she passed on the business cards he had left at her desk. It seemed that Nick Martin's work was very popular indeed and someone had advertised the fact that his work was in The Black Cat Gallery very effectively indeed.

As the countryside seemed to explode into life outside her home, with cherry blossom in the fields she passed and lambs in the fields, so Eleanor's life seemed to be coming to fruition. She felt that everything was beginning to fall into place.

By the end of two weeks she had almost sold out of his work and had altered the exhibition layout to cover the gaps that had been left where items had been sold. She knew that she should really contact Nick and ask for some more pieces, but she was afraid to speak to him now. Part of her thought that things couldn't get any worse, but another part of her kept thinking of several worse things that could happen. What if he turned up at the gallery with Kate? What if he tried to kiss her again now that she knew he had a fiancée? She couldn't risk it. Her heart felt as if it had taken all the beatings it could bear and she needed to protect herself. This man was not good news.

The last weekend of March looked as if it was going to be the wettest on record. The heavens opened and the rain poured down. Falling onto the already sodden ground it had nowhere to go and ran down the hill in cascades, collecting mud as it went. As Audrey had predicted, it looked like a flood was inevitable.

The rain hit the spring flowers hard, and the blossom was washed from the hawthorn trees, laying like forgotten confetti on the ground. The green shoots which had forced their way through up were now drowned in the waterlogged ground. The bright green of spring hope began to turn to the dirty brown of despair.

As the rain continued, the local news reports warned that the River Stour was getting increasingly high, and might be in danger of bursting its banks. Taking this with a pinch of salt, Eleanor assumed that the news crews were exaggerating for effect and took very little notice.

She did see that the car park had become covered with half an inch of water and that a large puddle had collected outside the back door. She had to leave the house by the front door when she needed to go outside, and was grateful for her funky purple wellies.

Rosie phoned to say that Stourton was in uproar. People were panic-buying and the shops were running out of food.

'It's ridiculous,' she said, 'It's just a little bit of water! I'll pop over later. I managed to snap up some crumpets before the starving natives got to them and Daniel's with a client, so we can have a leisurely afternoon tea today – just like ladies that lunch – or in this case eat crumpets.'

Eleanor laughed, 'Oh, do stop rambling and get off the phone, I can hear Darwin outside and need to go and let him in.'

As she opened the front door, a very wet Darwin shot in and ran up the stairs. This was unusual for him, as he usually went to the kitchen to see if he could scrounge a snack before settling down on her bed. She shrugged and let him go, thinking that she would make some scones to go with the crumpets to make a real treat for Rosie when she arrived.

The kitchen was dark for the time of day, with the rainclouds blocking out what little light there was and she had to turn on the light to see what she was doing. Looking out of the window, she saw a car driving into the yard with a horsebox in tow. She took one step back so that the driver couldn't see her. Who would be coming out in weather like this?

As she watched, Nick got out of the car and started to coax a frightened bay mare out of the horsebox.

Slipping on her wellington boots and raincoat, she stomped across towards him.

'What are you doing?' she shouted over the sound of the rain and the wind. Her hair whipped around her face and she had to hold it out of the way with one hand.

Nick turned round at the sound of her voice. His eyes were wide and his hair was plastered to his head by the rain. Their eyes locked for what seemed like minutes, but must only have been seconds. He drew a long shuddering breath, as if seeing her had relaxed him, and his shoulders dropped.

Feeling the horse pulling away from him, he started to lead her towards the stable block.

'Our stables are flooded. I needed to get Lady out. This is the only place I could think of,' came his unlikely explanation to Eleanor's question.

'Flooded?'

'Yes, the whole of the east side of Stourton is slowly going under water. The river is up to its banks and we're only about six inches away from a real flood.'

Eleanor stared, not knowing what to say. She knew Nick must be thinking of the day he lost his brother.

As she watched, the horse once more pulled at the reins, frightened by the unnatural light and the sound of the wind. Nick was pulled off his balance and in a second Lady backed away from him, her eyes wide and her teeth bared. The reins slipped through his fingers and she was free, standing motionless while she decided which way to run.

Without thinking, Eleanor lunged forwards and grabbed the reins. Lady reared at the unexpected movement and all but pulled Eleanor off the ground. It happened in a flash, and in the same instant that Eleanor felt the sharp stab of pain in her shoulder, she felt Nick's arms around her. One arm held her firmly around the waist, while the other reached up for the reins, his hand around hers.

Eleanor held her breath as the wind and the rain faded into the background. The only thing that she was aware of was the warm strength of Nick's body against hers and the powerful grasp of his hand as he gathered in the reins. Did she only imagine that he leant forward to breathe in the smell of her hair? Or that he held her for a split-second longer than he needed to?

As soon as the mare was captured, Nick soothed her with soft words and led her into one of the stables. He pushed shut the broken door, closing it as well as he could by wedging it shut with a piece of scrap timber.

Working fast and with his normal economy of movement, he uncoupled the horse box and jumped back into his car.

'Can you look after her for me?' he called from the car window and drove off. The hood of her jacket had blown down and she was left standing in the middle of the yard next to the abandoned horse box getting wetter and wetter.

Stunned as she was by the news of the flood, Eleanor was elated that Nick had entrusted the welfare of his horse to her. Of all the people he could have gone to in this time of crisis, he had chosen her.

Shaking herself back to reality she raced back to the house and phoned Rosie.

'Is it true? Is everywhere flooded?'

'I'm at the shop now,' gasped Rosie, 'and yes, everywhere is swimming. If it goes down now it'll be OK, but it looks like more rain is forecast tomorrow. I've got to go – I'll speak to you later,' And she ended the call almost before she had finished speaking.

Logging on to her laptop, Eleanor checked out the weather forecast. More rain was indeed forecast and there was a flood alert out for the area.

By 4pm it was almost completely dark and the wind had increased. The heavy rain was now being blown almost horizontally by the blasts of wind. She wondered briefly when a wind became a storm, or even a tornado. Walking across the yard to see to Lady, she had to fight to stay upright, leaning into the wind, her eyes almost shut against the dust that was being forced into them.

She made sure the Lady was comfortable, put out more water, and filled the manger from the bale of hay Nick had thrown into the corner. She had very little idea of what she needed to do for the horse, but she knew that Nick would be back to check on her soon. If there was a problem she would phone Audrey.

She stayed and petted the skittish horse for a while, scratching her ears and stroking her soft nose. Leaning her face against Lady's side, she trembled as she thought of

Nick's thighs pressed there, imagining that the warmth she felt was the residual warmth from his body.

'Are you going to be OK in here?' she asked the horse, 'I'm sorry we're not really set up for horses, but I think you'll be OK. I'm sure he'll be back for you soon.'

She secured the door and went back indoors.

Unsure of where to go or who to help, she stayed in the gallery. Although she felt helpless, she didn't want to block up the roads when emergency vehicles might be trying to get past, and she knew that even a small accident on these narrow country roads would make a huge difference to whether or not cars could get past.

She wandered around the house, looking alternately out of the front and back windows. As the evening work on, she realised that she had pulled something in her shoulder. She ran herself a hot bath and soaked for a while, but she couldn't fully relax. Drying herself, she dressed in pyjamas and a dressing-gown and resumed her arbitrary wandering.

Nick didn't come back and at 10 o'clock she took a cup of tea up to bed and read her new Katie fford book until she fell asleep, hoping that the storm would blow itself out.

She woke several times during the night to the sound of broken branches being thrown against the windows. Once she thought she heard the drone of a car coming down the lane, but by the time she was fully awake the sound had stopped.

The odd sounds she could hear coming from outside were drowned by the singing of the wind. Tommy the cat burrowed under the covers and she was grateful for the warmth of another living being. She listened to the wind whistling through the trees and fell asleep.

In the morning, she awoke to find that the storm had passed. The sky was a milky shade of blue and the sun was shining. She could hear the birdsong in the trees, and threw back the curtains to see what had happened.

Looking out of her window, Eleanor found it hard to believe what she saw.

Chapter Sixteen

Lit as if by a thousand fairy lights, her yard and garden were hardly recognisable as sunlight glanced off the raindrops still running down the leaves and across the ground. The large ash tree that normally stood to one side was now resting on top of the garden shed. The door to the end stable had blown off and a large branch had somehow wedged itself inside. Nick's horse box lay on one side. She was amazed that she had slept through most of it and not heard the noise it must all have made. Everywhere was covered with a layer of leaves and small branches.

She ran to the front window to check her car and was pleased to see it was still where she had parked it. With a frisson of excitement, she saw Nick's car parked next to it.

She wandered downstairs to make breakfast, and flicked on the lights, pleased to see that the electricity hadn't gone out. She fed the cat and turned on the kettle, wondering if she should go into village, and if so, where she should go to offer help. Perhaps Rosie's shop would be a good place to start.

As she stood at the sink, washing up a few things from the night before, she heard a sound in the stables. Thinking that the horse was escaping she ran outside and came face to face with Nick.

He was filthy dirty and had straw in his hair, but she had never seen him looking more appealing. His hair was still wet and hung in rats-tails around his neck, with that one strand still hanging loose. He pushed it back wearily, and she saw from his eyes that he probably hadn't been to sleep that night. He had in his aspect a raw manliness that she was finding irresistible. She was suddenly very aware that she stood before him in just her pyjamas and a dressing gown.

'Could I use your toilet?' he asked, looking at her as a shipwrecked sailor looks at a raft. 'I had to stay with Lady last night. The storm was frightening her.'

'Of course,' she pulled her dressing gown more tightly across her chest, 'You look as if you could do with a shower as well. You can if you want …' She waved a hand at house offering the use of it. Subconsciously, she was also offering herself, although consciously she thought no further than coming to his aid when he needed her.

He looked down at his clothes. 'I'd like to, but I can't put these on again afterwards.'

She was rather surprised that he agreed, expecting him to make his excuses and leave. It seemed that he was so tired he wasn't thinking straight.

'There's a shower in the downstairs loo just along the hall on your left. Throw the clothes out and I'll put them through the washer-dryer.'

As he threw his clothes out of the bathroom door, she tried not to think about him naked in her shower just inches away from where she stood. She definitely didn't want to think about the rivers of foaming shower gel running down his body. Bundling his clothes together, she walked slowly to the utility room, holding them to her face. Still slightly warm from his body, she could smell his scent through the pungent tang of mud and horse.

She turned on the washing machine and heard the shower running. Racing upstairs, she cleaned her teeth and washed her face. She then found Justin's dressing-gown at the back of her wardrobe, which she laid on the floor outside the shower room. She knocked on the door to let Nick know it was there.

She made coffee and toast and laid the table for breakfast, making sure that every detail was perfect. When Nick had finished his shower, he walked silently into the kitchen and sat down, looking across the table at her.

She poured coffee into the mug in front of him and offered the toast. He took a piece and they smiled across the table at each other like an old married couple. Her heart was racing, but there was still one thing eating away at her.

'I hope Kate won't mind you having breakfast with me. Perhaps you'd better not tell her.'

'Why should Kate mind?'

'Well, finding out that your fiancé is having breakfast with another woman is normally enough to make a woman mad. So I understand. I don't mean I've had any experience...,' she tailed off her sentence, enable to read the expression on his face.

'Eleanor, Kate's my sister.'

Eleanor stared. 'Your....'

'Yes, she's back in the UK to talk about the plans for the development. The reason I haven't been around is that I wanted to spend as much time with her as I could before she has to fly back.'

'To Australia.'

'Yes.'

'Where you're going to live.'

His face dropped. 'Well, things aren't finalised yet,' he said carefully. Then he chuckled, shaking his head, 'Did you really think she was my girlfriend? Wait till I tell her!' It was one of the few times she had seen him smile and it melted her heart. His eyes sparkled and he lifted his chin as he laughed, exposing the soft skin of his neck.

Getting up from his place at the table he walked over to Eleanor, dragging the blanket with him. 'Come here,' he said, putting out his hands.

'Things have really got off to a rough start with us, I know. And yes, I might be going to Australia. But that doesn't stop us making the most of what time we have, does it?'

She put her hands in his as she stood up and he held onto them as he pulled her towards him.

'The first thing we're going to have to talk about are these teddy pyjamas,'

She opened her mouth to protest, but was silenced by his kiss.

It was a long time before they spoke again and by the time they were ready to continue with their breakfast the coffee had gone cold.

An hour later they were both fed, dressed and ready to go. Nick had asked Eleanor to go with him to the farm to see what damage had been done the night before. Feeling as if there was nowhere she should be apart from at his side, she had, of course, agreed.

The day was like no other she had ever experienced. The level of devastation was incredible and the hard work that was being put into recovery was phenomenal. It was at times like this that being part of a small community really paid dividends, as friends and neighbours all worked together to help each other.

The radio station played a part in the recovery by broadcasting phone calls from people who needed help or who were worried about loved ones that couldn't be reached. Many of the roads were now impassable and it was impossible to get from one side of the river to the other as the bridge had been declared unsafe. The phone signals, which were patchy at the best of times in this area, were frustratingly unreliable, dropping calls at the worst of times.

Nick and Eleanor's first stop was Stourton Park Farm. The lower fields were under water, which was cause for concern in the long term, but did not pose an immediate threat. The house was far enough up the hill to have missed most of the floodwater, but some of the barns had suffered.

Nick's workshop was one of the buildings that had been hit badly. A tree had fallen across the roof, loosening the tiles. As the tiles had been lifted by the wind, rainwater had got in and soaked everything inside.

After making sure Mr and Mrs Preston were unhurt, Nick took time to spend a few minutes alone with his parents while Eleanor waited in the car, and she chose not to ask why. The whole village was in an uproar. Although the water from the flash flood had receded, the streets were covered in debris of all kinds and water pooled in every dip and behind every wall. The drains were awash and water was being forced up the pipes instead of down.

Police with loud hailers advised people to leave the area if they could and return when the waters had gone down further. People who were stuck their homes were advised to phone someone to let them know they were there, or signal from their windows to the passing patrols.

Nick's Land Rover was the perfect vehicle to use in the rescue operation, as it rode safely over most of the debris in its path and through the accumulated water. He quickly contacted the person in charge, who had set up camp in the Village Hall and they offered their services to ferry people out of their homes.

With his normal economy of words, he nodded to Eleanor to get into the car. It seemed natural that they should stay together, but she realised that she would be of more help at the Control Point.

She hesitated. 'No, I'll stay here. I'll only take up room that someone else might need.'

As she watched him drive off, she felt a strange sensation in her chest, as if part of her were being dragged out to be with him. She almost ran out into the road and called after him to stop. Instead, she pulled her coat tightly around her and pressed her hand to her heart. Her lips tight, she took a deep breath and turned away from the sight of his vanishing car.

Chapter Seventeen

The day was hectic and she didn't see Nick again until gone three o'clock. The light had almost gone, but working together the emergency rescue team had moved almost everybody out of the affected area. Eleanor had stayed at the checkpoint making tea, giving out information and sending people on their way happier than they had arrived. Her calm efficiency was a bonus to the team, and she was heaped with constant praise as she repeatedly saw a potential problem before it happened and averted it.

At the end of the day she saw Nick come into the room before he saw her. He looked as if he was wet through, his shoulders slumped. She saw him dragging his feet, and at first she thought he was injured, but then she realised that he was just so tired that he couldn't lift them. She knew that he had had little sleep the night before and could see that he was completely exhausted.

He looked around and caught sight of Eleanor. Walking across to her he silently put his arms around her and rested his chin on her head. She briefly closed her eyes and felt him relax into her.

'Home?' she whispered, although she already felt at home in his arms and knew that from now on 'home' would be wherever he was.

He still didn't speak, but just led her out to the car and opened the door for her to get in, closed it behind her.

Walking round to the driver's door, he looked as if he hardly had the strength to climb in, and she almost asked what he had done that day. She stopped herself, not wanting to break the spell, and wondered if she would ever know. She knew how much harder it must have been for him than for anyone else.

Before they could get into the car, however, one of the men who had been working with Nick called him back.

'Nick!' he looked as exhausted as Nick did himself, 'I've just spoken to Ron. He says the Philpott children have been left at Broad Oak Farm on their own. Mum popped out to the shops and can't get back to them because the bridge is down. She's distraught, poor thing,' he shook his head, looking as if he were hardly able to take any more, 'Is there any way you could take a run over there and see if they're all right?'

Nick didn't hesitate, 'How many children?' he asked.

'Four,' came the reply, 'Lauren's fourteen - she was left in charge - the girls are eight and five and Bobby's two.'

Nick looked at Eleanor to confirm what he already knew.

'We'll go straight there,' she said, climbing into the car.

Driving in the half-light of early dusk was hard enough, but now it had begun to rain again. Not the hard, pounding rain of the night before, but hard enough to make driving difficult.

Nick navigated through the debris with skill, his knowledge of the area a blessing, as they had to keep detouring to avoid roads that were blocked by fallen trees. The narrow country lanes had no signposts, and only a local man would know where he was going.

They passed near to the river at one point, and saw how swollen it had become. The normally clear water had dragged up silt from the bottom as it swirled on its way and it was now cloudy and foreboding. It had picked up broken branches and leaves and they spun along with alarming speed, collecting leaves and litter as they went. No wonder the supports to the bridge had been damaged.

As they approached Broad Oak Farm they saw light coming from the window.

'Look!' shouted Eleanor above the noise of the wind and the rain, 'They're all right!'

Nick nodded once but kept his eyes on the road.

'Let's hope so.'

They pulled to a stop in front of the farmhouse and banged on the door.

'Lauren! We've come to help you! Open up!'

The door flew open and a petite girl in a huge jacket and knitted hat opened the door. She was carrying a crying toddler who was also swaddled in clothes several sizes too large for him.

'Mum?' was the first thing she said, looking behind them into the car. Tears and dirt streaked her face.

Nick and Eleanor gently pushed her back into the house and closed the door. Once inside, they could see that the light had come from an open fire that had been lit in the living room. Two other children huddled under a duvet on the sofa, clinging to one another.

'Where's Mummy?' was the first question they asked, and Eleanor felt a pang of pity.

'Everything's going to be OK,' she said, taking the toddler from the girl, 'Mummy can't come home at the moment because she's on the other side of the river.' She looked around the room. 'Is your electricity off?'

'Yes,' replied the older girl, 'It went off last night. Mum went to buy some more coal and we've been waiting for her to come back,' her lower lip began to tremble, 'I fed them as well as I could and I kept the fire going to keep them warm...'

Now that an adult had arrived, it seemed that her small reserve of courage had run out. She burst into tears and sat down on the sofa, pulling her sisters towards her.

Nick damped down the fire and Eleanor got the children up, checking that they had warm clothes on.

'Lauren, can you go and pack a bag with some clothes and stuff in?' Lauren looked blank at the mention of a bag, so Eleanor continued 'I'll get some carrier bags. Can you find their favourite clothes to take with them? You might have to stay with someone else for a few days.'

The three girls all looked worried at this news, so Eleanor gave the two younger ones the task of finding their shoes and choosing a toy each as well as one for their little brother, Bobby. This kept them busy while Nick walked around the house making sure it was secure.

Mindful of the fact that driving would be even more dangerous once it was fully dark, they hurried to get the children into the car, stowing the bags of clothes in the back and letting them carry their favourite toy.

The journey back was indeed treacherous. Although the rain had not increased, the wind had picked up and they could feel it battering the car as they drove through the open roads.

Eleanor rode in the front of the car, and the four children all piled into the back. They had no car seat for the toddler, but decided against strapping him in. He sat on his sister's lap, still whimpering as he picked up the fear on the faces of his siblings.

Nick drove slowly, anticipating the bends in the roads and manoeuvring carefully around obstacles. They could see the lights of Stourton below them as they passed the river and were just beginning to believe they could make it without incident when there was a loud bang and the car lurched to one side. Everyone was thrown to one side, and the car came to rest at an angle half-way up a bank.

Stunned, they sat in silence for a while before the children all started to cry at once. Even Eleanor felt like sobbing with the shock, but she knew that she had to remain strong.

'Goodness, that was a surprise! Is everyone alright?' she called into the back of the vehicle.

'I've dropped Milly,' came one little voice, but apart from that there appeared to be no injuries. Even Bobby, who had fallen off his sister's lap.

Nick took control. 'OK. If you've bumped your head, give it a good rub, but we have to get out if the car,' he told them. 'Eleanor, can you look on the floor for her doll?'

They got out and took stock of the situation. The car had struck a pothole and burst a tyre. It was now embedded into the side of a willow tree.

'We're going to have to walk the rest of the way' was the verdict.

Nick picked up the little boy and made sure each of the girls had a toy to carry so that they had something to distract them from the situation they were in. 'Come on, the sooner we started, the sooner we'll be there.'

They made a sorry little parade, trudging through the mud, with their hair alternately lifted by the wind and flattened by the rain. After a while they gave up avoiding the rivers of rainwater that crossed their way, and trudged on in silence.

Eleanor was impressed by the way the children had risen to the challenge and was just about to say so when the toddler let out an almighty scream. Nick looked horrified, and held the struggling boy away from him as if he might have done something to hurt the little lad.

'Tedda!' shouted the boy, 'Tedda!!'

Lauren stepped forward and spoke to her brother, 'Where's Tedda?' she asked him, looking around to see if the teddy bear had been dropped on the ground.

The boy screamed again, banging his head backwards into Nick, who was having a hard job keeping hold of him. He knew from experience how hard a blow from a toddler's head could be. He put the boy down but without warning Bobby pulled away from him and darted away and ran towards the river. Too late, they noticed the teddy bear caught on a log at the river's edge, where the boy must have thrown it.

'No!' they all shouted at once, but it was too late. Nick ran forward to stop him, and although he managed to catch the boy before he got to the river, he lost his footing and the two of them fell sideways into the churning water. The girls watched in horror as Nick clung to the log, holding the boy's head out of the water.

'Eleanor!' he gasped, 'Take him!' The swirling water was pulling at his legs and Eleanor guessed that there was a strong undercurrent. She could see that he was struggling.

Holding onto a tree branch, she slid down the bank towards the water and reached for the boy. Although she could touch him, she couldn't get a firm enough hold to pull him back out of danger.

'Lauren, quick!' she shouted, 'Come and help! Let me hold your legs while you get Bobby.'

Lauren slithered down beside Eleanor and lay in the mud, reaching out for her brother.

Between them, they managed to get the child on the bank, and Lauren hugged tightly him as she carried him back to the main path. Eleanor could see that Nick was beginning to tire, and he was shaking with the cold.

'Nick,' she called to him, 'Look at me.' The brown eyes lifted to hers and a look of hope came into his face. 'Don't you dare let go,' she told him, leaning forward. He tightened his hold on the log and flicked his dripping hair out of his eyes, but only seconds later his head drooped, and he only lifted when his face hit the water.

'Nicholas Preston! Look at me!' she shouted again, reaching out to him. He lifted his head and their eyes locked. Pulling himself up along the fallen log, he moved slowly towards her until she could grab his wrist. His eyes never left her face as she put her whole weight against his and started to lift him out of the water. Within minutes they were both lying against a tree, panting.

As they lay there, wondering what their next move would be, they heard the sound of an engine and Lauren's voice as she shouted to the van to stop. Two of the men who had been working at the community centre came and helped Nick into the car and Eleanor and the children all squashed into the back seats together.

The children were taken to the community centre where their mother was waiting, and Nick and Eleanor were dropped off at The Black Cat. It all happened so fast that they hardly had time to think.

Letting themselves in through the back door, they dropped their muddy outer clothing on the floor and left it where it fell. Eleanor led Nick up the stairs to her room and pulled back the quilt. It seemed like the most natural thing in the world for him to stay with her as he stepped out of his wet clothes and sat on the edge of the bed.

'Eleanor...' he began, reaching out for her.

'Shhhh....' She gave him a gently push. He fell back onto the pillows and she moved the lock of hair to kiss his forehead. By the time she stood up he was sound asleep.

Chapter Eighteen

The next day Eleanor awoke to the smell of bacon frying. Not knowing how fast their relationship was going to develop, she had slept in the spare bedroom, much to the disgust of Tommy the cat, who had seemed rather confused. After sniffing around the spare room for a while he had chosen to go back to his normal place at the end of her bed and had slept with Nick.

Eleanor dressed and showered quickly before making her way downstairs. New jeans were teamed with a chunky jumper and a plain gold chain. She had towel-dried her hair for speed, and had now decided that the tousled look suited her. Her face was scrubbed clean and was free of makeup. The smile on her face was all the enhancement it needed.

'Look, no teddy pyjamas today,' she grinned as she walked into the kitchen.

Nick looked up. His hair was still wet from his morning shower, and he had managed to find clean clothes from somewhere.

'I was up early to see to Lady, so I went home and changed,' he explained. He waved a hand at the breakfast things, 'You don't mind me...'

'No, of course not.' They skirted round each other like anxious foals just introduced into the same field. In a curious exchange of roles, Eleanor sat down at her own kitchen table and waited to be served. She noticed that he had managed to find the coffee maker and had put a pot of coffee on to brew.

Now that the excitement of the previous day had gone, they were both unsure how to proceed. The kiss from the day before seemed so far away now, and had been eclipsed by the events that followed. There was so much left to say, but the words were left unspoken. Eleanor knew that her heart was now fully committed to this relationship, but she was worried that her head had yet to follow suit.

Nick put a full English breakfast in front of her and sat down.

'About yesterday...' he started, not meeting her eyes.

137

Eleanor froze. She could see by the regret in his face what it was he was about to say. How could she have been so wrong? She smiled, 'Hey, don't say a thing. You're welcome. I just did what I needed to.'

She dropped her eyes to her plate and forced down a few mouthfuls. 'You know, after yesterday, I don't think I can eat all this. I'm awfully sorry.' She pushed back her chair, wincing as she twisted her injured shoulder.

Nick stood and reached out towards her. 'Eleanor, let's talk about this.'

She stepped back out of his reach and grabbed her coat from the back of the sofa, holding in front of her like a shield. Her breath was coming in shaky gasps and she could feel that her eyes were wide. One part of her wanted to scream at him and say the most hurtful things she could think of, and another wanted to hold onto him and beg him to love her.

She stood for a moment, tears brimming in her eyes. She pressed her lips together to stop their trembling and raised her hand to cover them. She had to take a deep breath before she spoke.

'I'm going to check on Rosie. Please lock the door when you leave.'

She grabbed her keys and all but ran out of the door. Thrusting the key into the ignition, she turned it roughly and was thankful to hear the engine start. Spinning her wheels on the gravel, she sped out of the driveway and down the road. Realising she was travelling too fast for the single-track carriageway she pulled into the next lay-by.

She wound down her window to let in the cold morning air and looked out over the Kentish countryside. The view was stunning. The trees and hedgerows seemed to have soaked up the rain like sponges and grown by several inches overnight. The sunlight shone on the bright new growth of the crops and birds sang in the skies.

Sitting in the driver's seat Eleanor dropped her hands to her lap and felt the tears rolling down her face. On her own in the middle of nowhere, there was no-one to see or hear her, so she let herself sob.

As she calmed herself, she dug in her pocket for a paper tissue and wiped her face. Why had she allowed herself to get in this state? She had only known the man a few months, and had only been kissed by him twice. The memory of those kisses brought on fresh tears. She had been so sure of his strength and loyalty and could not believe that he had meant nothing by his actions.

She calmed herself down and waited by the roadside until the rear view mirror showed that her face was no longer red, and then drove into village.

Far from seeing the normal bustling crowd, there were only one or two people in the streets. Most people had been evacuated the day before and only a few shop-keepers had returned today to see what damage had been done. Rosie was one of these.

The mud and debris had flooded the lower floors of every house on the High Street, and Rosie's shop was no exception.

'Eleanor!' she exclaimed, 'What are you doing here? Why aren't you sorting out the gallery? Is it badly damaged?' She, too, looked as if she hadn't had much sleep the night before.

'I'm on a hill up there, don't forget, and the gallery didn't flood at all.' Eleanor looked round the shop and felt a pang of guilt that her own business had escaped unharmed.

Rosie sat down on a chair and quickly got up again, rubbing the damp from her skirt. She started to move some of the smaller stock items into plastic storage boxes, ready to be moved out of the shop.

'Everything here is sodden. Even the things that didn't come in direct contact with the flood water have gradually soaked it up.' She pushed back her hair and shook her head. 'It's going to take ages to get back to normal. Thank goodness Daniel made me take out the higher level of insurance.'

139

'What about your house,' asked Eleanor, 'Did that get flooded?'

'No, we're OK over there. Come back with me and tell me what happened to you yesterday. Someone told me you were helping out and that you went home with Nick Preston. Is that right?'

Eleanor's resolve began to crumble and she could feel the tears begin to well up again. Pressing her lips together to stop her chin from trembling, she turned her head away and shrugged.

'No, they must have been mistaken,' she lied.

Rosie put her hand on her friends arm and was about to challenge her when they heard Audrey's voice outside in the street. She was calling for Darwin.

'Audrey!' they called in unison. The older lady splashed across to them, looking very unlike her usual, beautifully-groomed self. It looked to Eleanor as if she had been crying, too. They drew her into the shop, found her a dry chair to sit on and asked her what the matter was.

'I can't find Darwin,' she explained, her voice higher than usual, as if she was on the edge of hysteria. 'I've been up to the gallery, but I couldn't get in,' she looked at Eleanor, 'I rang the bell but nobody answered.'

Eleanor felt a stab of regret. That meant that Nick had gone, too.

'I'll go and look now. Do you want to follow in your car, or shall I just go and check and call you?

Audrey thought for a moment. 'Can I come too? I've looked everywhere and there's nowhere else I can think of.'

She looked devastated at the thought that Darwin might be lost, or worse, and Eleanor's heart went out to her. 'I'm sure he'll be there. Why don't you come too, Rosie, and we'll have tea there instead of at yours.'

The three ladies each drove their own car up the hill to the gallery. As she rounded the corner, Eleanor's heart beat faster and her mouth went dry. What if Nick was still there?

His car was gone from the car park, however, and the house was quiet.

As soon as she opened the door, Audrey started to call for her cat, and each of the three companions moved off in a different direction to look for the animal. They had only been in the house a few minutes when they heard Audrey's tone of voice change.

'Darwin!' They knew by the loving tone that the cat had been found. Her next words 'Oh, you naughty boy,' were muffled, and her friends knew that this was because her face was buried in his thick fur. They each knew that they would have done the same. Eleanor picked up Tommy and held him close, glad that he had been here all the time and not been caught out in the storm.

Over tea and biscuits, the friends discussed what effect the flood damage was going to have on Stourton.

'I hear the Village Hall is completely wrecked,' said Rosie, 'The water got in underneath the back door and the parquet flooring in ruined.'

Audrey's 'No!' seemed out of proportion to the information. 'It's the Art About Town fundraising exhibition in two weeks' time. We won't be able to have it.' Having recovered her composure once they had found Darwin, she suddenly seemed to drop once again into despair.

'Well, that's easily solved,' said Rosie, feeding pieces of shortbread biscuit to the cats, 'Use the gallery here.'

It seemed so simple. Slightly worried that the out-of-town venue wouldn't be as good as the Village Hall, it was nevertheless the only alternative venue in Stourton.

'I'll put it to the committee then,' said Audrey, 'And I'll get back to you just as soon as I can.' Her mood once again lifted, and she looked immediately younger.

The woman who left was hardly recognisable as the person who had been searching for her lost cat just an hour ago. She now seemed full of her normal vigour and pounced on Darwin as he made a dash for the cat flap. 'Oh no you don't!' she scolded him, 'You're coming home with me. Come and get into the car.'

After she had gone, Rosie gently probed Eleanor on the question of Nick, but she stopped as soon as she saw the distress on Eleanor's face. It wasn't just that she was interested in what was going on in Eleanor's life; she could sense that something wasn't going the way Eleanor would like, and she wanted to offer to help. With her big heart and comforting appearance, she was always a huge help in any crisis situation. She had first met many of her friends when she had stepped in to help them at a crossroads in their lives.

Wandering around the gallery, she again commented on the standard of Nick's work.

'This stuff is really good, isn't it?' she stopped to look at a trio of ducklings tucked under the wings of their mother, 'He really captures the essence of each animal. Which ones do you like best?'

The initial drawings that were displayed alongside some of the pieces showed such sensitivity and delicacy of line that they could only have been produced by someone with a deep love of nature as well as a genuine artistic skill. The sketchbooks on display were filled with doodles and notes that showed they had been inspired by long and patient hours of watching the flowers and animals they represented.

When Rosie had finished flicking through the sketchbooks, she went into the Small Gallery, as it was now called. She moved a few bits and pieces around, creating a new display area with some straw and baskets that Eleanor had brought in to help emphasise the rural nature of the goods. She had also picked up some gingham tea towels, which made the home-made jams and pickles look as if they were part of a picnic lunch. Bunches of wildflowers in jam jars added to the effect.

'If you want anything else to go in this gallery,' she said, 'I know a great shop in Stourton with a load of flood-damaged stock.' Standing with her hands up to her head, she held her hair back off her face. 'Actually, that's a fabulous idea!'

'What?' teased her friend, 'Having it all cut off?'

Rosie looked confused for a moment, then grinned when she got the joke, 'No, I'll hire the Craft Gallery while the shop dries out. You could move the seating out of the conservatory and put this lot out there. If it works out well, it can be my second shop.'

Eleanor looked around her, imaging what it might look like. Rosie's pottery had sold well when it was in the main gallery, and people would very probably come back looking for more. Customers were creatures of habit and liked to collect pieces by artists they knew. Once they had started buying pieces by one person, they tended to buy more over the years.

'These shelving units will be perfect for displaying the kitchen ware, and if you don't mind I could keep some of the jars in here to make it look like a farmhouse kitchen.' Eleanor agreed that it was a fabulous idea.

'The only tiny little flaw in that plan is that this isn't a permanent set-up,' she reminded Rosie, 'Don't forget that my lease runs out this summer. This was just a pilot project to see if I could make it work. This is all going to be bulldozed in August.'

Chapter Nineteen

Stourton was never quite the same after the flood and neither was Eleanor's life. After the disastrous events of the night of the storm, she had decided to steer clear of Nick Preston and anything to do with him. Thank goodness she had stayed in the spare room that night and not laid herself open to even more shame and regret.

Daniel had been offered work in Dubai, which meant that he would be away for at least six months, and although she would miss him, Rosie agreed that it he should take the job. She divided her time between the shop and The Black Cat Gallery, and as things turned out, she spent more and more time with Eleanor.

One sunny day she arrived with a new batch of pottery, this time glazed in a vibrant red with gold highlights.

'Goodness!' exclaimed Eleanor, 'That's a bit of a departure from your normal style.'

'I know,' replied Rosie, taking boxes from her car and stacking them inside the front door, 'I wanted to see how far I could push myself outside my comfort zone.' She unwrapped a large ginger jar which glowed with the colours of a vivid sunset. The splatter of gold patterning seemed to flow down the side of the vessel like liquid sunlight, and as it caught the rays of the afternoon sun through the window, glowed as if lit from within.

The two women laid out the new pieces and Eleanor helped Rosie to decide how to display them. They worked well together, each one seeming to know what the other needed before they asked for it. When the display was almost finished, Eleanor said.

'I was going to make tea, but it's just occurred to me that a glass of wine would be nice. I'll make some sandwiches and we can sit in the kitchen and listen for the gallery bell while we eat.'

Rosie agreed, and they settled down at the old kitchen table to gossip, as friends do.

The afternoon wore on, and while Eleanor made a pot of tea, Rosie talked to some visitors in the gallery. She came back into the room with a very smug look on her face.

'They bought something didn't they?' asked Eleanor. ' Come on, spill the beans.'

Rosie waved a handful of £10 notes at her. 'They said they loved the new work, and bought two pieces,' she crowed. 'Whoohoo!'

***

The Craft Gallery was now The Blue Moon Gallery and Rosie's own pottery pieces had pride of place. Having the two galleries in one place doubled the amount of visitors that each had, and sales were high. The opening of the new gallery space had been a good excuse to put out another press release, and the newspaper had been very happy to take some snaps of the personable and photogenic Rosie McAlister with her beautiful pots.

The Art About Town exhibition always attracted a lot of visitors and had gone well. There had been one or two awkward moments for Eleanor when Nick's mother had brought guests to view the work, but on the whole she had managed to avoid both Nick and the rest of his family. Even Lady had returned to her own stable.

As the year wore on, Rosie and Eleanor kept the galleries going by creating a series of seasonal events to draw it he visitors, with Easter being a major project.

Spring came and the vibrant colours of the late-flowering bulbs were a welcome sight when they appeared. Rosie drew Eleanor's attention to the first cuckoo of the year when she heard it, and Eleanor was reminded of the cyclical nature of life in the countryside. The old Eleanor would never have waited a whole year to hear the first call of a single bird.

Rosie's shop was almost back to normal now, after an initial hiccup with the insurance claim, but she was still living at the gallery and devoted a lot of her time to helping Eleanor. They worked together on projects which promoted the two galleries and which enhanced the careers of both ladies.

Hoping that the Easter Bank Holiday would be fine, they arranged an Easter exhibition featuring the artwork of local school children and put on an Easter Egg Hunt in the garden. Allowing the children to add decorations to their own cupcakes had been a fantastic idea of Rosie's, and everyone was having a great time.

During the afternoon Eleanor took a five-minute break and was sitting in the courtyard garden when a couple from out of town walked past. She was flicking through a magazine and concentrated on licking the icing off her cupcake, enjoying the sight of the daffodils as they danced in the breeze. The couple came to a stop a few yards away from Eleanor and didn't seem to see her. Idly listening to their conversation, she heard them agree with each other that this would make a great spot to sit and paint the view.

She was interrupted in her consideration of this thought by a commotion at the cupcake stall. She deftly averted complete mayhem by producing another container of stars-shaped sprinkles and the conversation in the garden was forgotten.

As the sun began to go down, Eleanor was feeling as happy as she could do. The day had been a great success; it had been unseasonably warm and several people had taken the time to congratulate her on the way of the gallery had turned out. Perhaps she had made a success of this venture after all. Her happiness was short-lived.

As she pottered around the garden, clearing up , the tell-tale scrunch of gravel let her know that a new visitor had arrived and she looked up to see Nick walking towards her. Glancing around like a rabbit caught in the headlights she realised that she had nowhere to go and that she would have to speak to him.

She waited for him to speak first.

'Come on,' he reached out a hand to her.

'Sorry?'

'Get in the car. There's something I want to show you.'

Eleanor grabbed a cardigan and locked up the gallery while Nick started the car.

They drove in silence, with Nick concentrating on the road and Eleanor looking pointedly out of the window. She desperately wanted him to kiss her again, but was afraid to let herself get drawn into a relationship that could only end in separation. The roads became narrower as they travelled deep into the countryside.

Eventually, Eleanor had to ask, 'Where are we going?'

'Just wait and see.' His deep voice reverberated into her and the echo of it stayed in her mind. It sounded like a promise of something spectacular, so she waited with as much patience as she could.

They came to a small car park and Nick pulled the car to a stop. 'We have to walk from here.' Looking around Eleanor could see the back of a housing estate and a badly-kept car park. There were no obvious signs of anything worth seeing here.

'Where are we going?'

'Somewhere really special. My Dad used to bring us here as children. He told us that is was a magical place and that whenever anything was wrong you could come here and it would be taken away. I think he was just telling us a story, but my sister and I always used to come here when we needed to refuel. It's just...calming.'

As Eleanor listened she realised that she knew very little about Nick as a person. Her feelings towards him were based on animal instinct as much as anything, not long acquaintanceship, as many relationships are. She wondered if what she felt counted as love at first sight.

Nick led her along a series of narrow paths, until they entered a wooded area. The evening light had almost fully disappeared and Nick glanced at the sky, 'Hurry up or we'll miss it.' The followed the path through the woods, stumbling occasionally on roots across their path and avoiding the brambles the snaked out towards them.

As the woods started to thin out, Nick stopped, 'Do you trust me?' She hesitated, wondering what was going to happen, 'Yes.' She was very aware that they were completely alone in the middle of nowhere and that there was nobody within earshot. To her surprise, she realised that she did trust him; completely and utterly. If he asked, she would follow him anywhere.

'Shut your eyes, then. We're going up that slope there, so watch where you put your feet.'

Eleanor did as she was asked, and felt his hands on her waist and felt her heart contract. She didn't have to be asked again to close her eyes. Fighting the urge to lean back into him, she walked slowly forwards. She felt the ground under them rise, and then flatten out. Nick took her by the shoulders and turned her to the side. 'Now open your eyes.'

Eleanor gasped. They had come out of the woods onto a hill and they stood in a clearing that contained a collection of standing stones. From where they stood they could see over miles and miles of darkening countryside.

The sun was almost down and the sky was painted in broad strokes of orange and neon pink, throwing long shadows across the land. As they watched, it dipped below the horizon and they were bathed in the strange half-light of dusk that comes before the deep blackness of night.

All around them they could hear the last songs of the birds on their way to their nests and the tinkle of wind chimes. Looking around, Eleanor saw that the trees surrounding the clearing had been decorated with ribbons and tokens by previous visitors.

'What is this place?' she breathed.

'It's an ancient place of worship,' he replied. 'I thought you'd like it. It would have been teeming with people yesterday, on the fourteenth, but I wanted to bring you here when it would be just us.'

He moved to stand behind her and put his arms around her. As she started to turn towards him, he stopped her, holding her close to stop her from turning.

'No. I have something to say and I can't say it when you look at me like that.'

'Like what?'

He was so close that he spoke into her hair, and she leaned back into him. 'Like a child who's lost a puppy,' he said, sadly.

She smiled, desperate to turn around, but wanting to do as he had asked. She nuzzled her head back under his chin and closed her eyes, waiting for him to finish so she could kiss him.

'I know you think I've been avoiding you,' he started, 'and I suppose I have. You must know how much I like you, but you know about Australia, and I know your lease is up this summer, and I just don't think it's a good idea for us to start a relationship right now.'

Again? She's been brought up here to this beautiful, magical spot and he'd let her down again?

'You're right, of course,' she agreed, hoping that her tone came across as cool and not childish,

'I don't know why we're even having this conversation. There's no reason we can't be friends,' she said, knowing that she could never be just friends with this man, when she wanted so badly to hold onto him and never let him go. 'Shall we go back now?'

Chapter Twenty

April segued into May and the fields began to take on their summer colours. Darkening as the foliage matured, the trees seemed to be sturdier. Orchards burst into blossom and whole fields looked as if they were covered in cherry-flavoured popcorn.

Walking through Stourton one day, Eleanor found herself looking at the Village Hall. After the flood, the insurance money had paid for basic repairs, but the town was still raising money for the improvements that were planned. Scaffolding poles stood like lost guards around the east end of the building.

Eleanor stopped to look at the posters in the window, seeing that many of the annual events had found new homes and were advertised as being in their new venues.

One poster that remained unchanged was the one for the Tuesday Art Group. This had been moved to a window that had the sign 'these events have been cancelled' displayed above it.

Eleanor remembered the Easter event at the gallery when she had overheard the conversation about the view from the gallery. Her mind began to whirr. Taking out her phone, she rang the number on the poster.

'Hello, is that the secretary of the Tuesday Art Group?' she asked.

The woman who had answered began to explain that the group had been temporarily cancelled, but Eleanor interrupted her.

'Actually, I'm phoning from The Black Cat Gallery and I wondered if your group would like to meet there for the next few weeks. It seems such a shame to cancel your meetings when I have the room available.'

'That does sound like an ideal solution,' agreed the lady, 'I don't want to sound like I'm looking a gift horse in the mouth, but can I just ask you a few questions?'

'Of course, it's always best to be up-front about things. Ask me anything you like.'

Eleanor described the room she had in mind, explained that the group would be able to look around the gallery while they were here, and reminded the lady about the location of the gallery, pointing out that the views would be perfect for painting outside, when the weather was good enough. There was plenty of parking, and most people knew where the gallery was, so it seemed an ideal solution.

They agreed that the group would have the use of an upstairs room and that Eleanor would provide refreshments. Of course, they would be painting and sketching outside if the weather was good, but they would pay for the hire of the room at their current rate, which Eleanor was pleased to agree to.

Eleanor cleared out one of the upstairs rooms that she had originally chosen not to use. When she had first taken on the lease of the house, she had only furnished a bedroom for herself and two spare bedrooms for guests, so there were several rooms upstairs that were still empty.

Clearing the room of the clutter that naturally accumulates, Eleanor found twelve chairs for the art group and an old dining table that had been in the garage. All it needed was a quick sand down and a layer of furniture wax to make it shine.

The chairs were mismatched, but the table looked great when Eleanor pushed it underneath the window and placed a huge jug of flowers in the middle. A few paintings and drawings from her own personal art collection added to the cosy, informal feel of the room. Although it was almost empty, the room felt welcoming and was just right for the art group's needs.

One of the gentlemen members that arrived assumed that they had hired one of the rooms in the stable block, and Eleanor had to run across and bring him back. Chatting as they crossed the yard, she realised that using the stable block as hirable rooms was a very good idea. There must be lots of groups that needed accommodation, especially now that the village hall was unavailable. She once more started to think that it might make good business sense to refurbish the stable block and advertise them for hire. If only the lease wasn't going to run out in a couple of months, it would be a fabulous idea.

The first meeting of the art group was a huge success. They met upstairs to go over club business, then all trooped outside to paint the view. After their refreshments they looked at the work in the gallery, glad to have like-minded people they could share their opinions with. The second part of the meeting was spent in the upstairs room finishing their paintings and chatting.

After they had left, Eleanor phoned Rosie to share her plan to develop the stable block but as they chatted she realised that as she only had a few more months left in the gallery, spending money on refurbishment would be money wasted.

***

Her friendship with Rosie had deepened, and Eleanor now regarded her as the sister she never had. Thinking about her plans for the future, she thought about having to leave the gallery and start again in a new location. She was beginning to think that this whole year had turned out to be rather disastrous.

The next Tuesday was a busy one, as the art group had invited a local celebrity to speak to them and they had asked Eleanor to put on an extra special afternoon tea. Using some of the local preserves, she baked a variety of small biscuits and a Kentish Apple Cake, which had become one of her specialities.

She set out the tea in the conservatory area of the gallery so that the group would have room to circulate and talk to their guest as they ate. Topping up the tea pot, she was surprised that the Secretary called her over to be introduced to the guest.

'This is Eleanor Stratton, our gallery owner,' she heard, 'We're all so proud of what she's done for art in the area. Before she came, we never really had a focus, but having the gallery here has drawn people in from all around and we're becoming quite well–known as a little artists' colony here.'

Eleanor demurred, but was secretly thrilled that people were happy with what she had achieved. It was just a pity that nobody said it to her directly, and that she had been suffering under the mistaken idea that she had failed in what she had been doing.

Another topic of conversation at the meeting was the lack of weekend art courses in the area. People exchanged stories of weekends they had spent in different parts of the country and of how successful many of them had been.

'What a shame you don't offer something like that here,' said one lady, 'It would be great to come here for a weekend.'

Her friend laughed, 'But you only live down the road,' she pointed out.

'Yes, but if there was a really good tutor, I could come during the day and go home at night. Mind you, if the dinners were going to be as good as this tea, I might stay overnight and save myself the washing up!'

Again, Eleanor was amazed that such a simple idea had been looming on the horizon and yet still been missed.

When the group left, she stayed up late with her laptop balanced on her knees, working out costs for weekend painting courses. Before she had finished, even Tommy had gone to bed.

The next morning, Eleanor looked again at the figures she had drawn up. They did show that the weekend art classes would make good business sense, but as with any new idea, they would take time to organise. They wouldn't just happen overnight. She would need to advertise the courses in national art magazines, which would take at least three months, taking into account their submission dates for adverts.

She saved the document in a folder she called 'Plans for the Future' and started to think instead about her plans for May Bank Holiday.

***

Three days later, as she was standing at the back door calling for Tommy, Nick drove round to the back yard, parked his car and walked across the yard towards her. He was dressed casually, as always, in a t-shirt and shorts, and he pushed his hair back as he walked towards her, holding up his hand against the sun to shield his eyes.

Her first thought had been that he might try to kiss her again, but she quickly put this thought to the back of her mind and tried to look unconcerned as he stopped in front of her. He stood a little further away than she had expected, as if he didn't trust himself to get too close to her. They both started to talk at once, then both stopped.

'You first,' said Eleanor, happy to listen to whatever he had to say. The deep cadence of his voice seemed to speak to something inside her, and she fixed her eyes onto his face as he spoke.

'I just came to tell you,' he started, looking down at the ground, 'That I'll definitely be going to Australia with my parents. We're going at the beginning of August for a holiday and if we can get the paperwork finalised, we'll stay out there.'

Eleanor took a small step backwards into the house. This was not what she had been expecting. Her breath seemed to stall in her chest and she put one hand onto the door frame to support herself. Not knowing what to say, she stayed silent for a while. They stood frozen for a minute, each waiting for the other to speak.

'Nick?'

When he looked up at her she saw on his face an expression of such pain that she could hardly stop herself from reaching out to him.

'I'm sorry, Eleanor. It shouldn't have been like this. My Mum and Dad....I can't leave them.'

154

For a moment, she thought that he was moving towards her, but he turned abruptly and walked towards the stable block and disappeared from view.

Eleanor stood where she was for a long time, remembering his voice, the way he stood and how he walked. Would this really be one of the last times she would see him? She thought briefly about running round to the studio and begging him to stay, but instead she ran a large bowl of hot water and started to mop the floor.

'Get out of the way, Tommy,' she said as the cat poked his nose through the cat flap, and mopped furiously in front of the door. Wrapped up in a confusion of feelings, she wanted to take time to work through the pain, and to try to make sense of it. Allowing herself the luxury of cuddling the cat and feeling sorry for herself would only encourage her to ignore what was happening.

As she relived the conversation in her head, she heard a huge clanging of metal as he threw tools and equipment into a box and she saw him again as he carried it to his car. The expression on his face as he drove away was unreadable.

Chapter Twenty-One

The first weekend of June was warm and sunny, and as the bees buzzed around the flowers, Eleanor started to think about moving on and to reflect on her time at the gallery.

The garden was full to bursting point with new growth and the hot air seemed heavy with fragrance and birdsong. Everything seemed to be coming to fruition except for her own personal life plans.

On one hand, she felt she had managed to accomplish a great deal. She had started a business from scratch which was making a profit after less than a year, which she felt was a significant achievement. Apart from Rosie and Audrey, whom she counted as 'best friends', she had a large circle of friends in Stourton that she knew she could count on whenever she needed to.

Her home was as near perfect as it could be, if you didn't count the fact that it was only leasehold, and Tommy made her home complete.

She stroked him as he lay on the sofa beside her, rubbing his ears in the way he liked, and knew that she was kidding herself. Lovely as he was, he was no substitute for a husband. Her heart ached as she thought of what her existence might be like with a partner to support her and to share the highs and lows of her life.

She wondered if she should have tried harder to work out her differences with Justin, but just as quickly put the thought out of her head. There was no way Justin would fit into her current life, and she now knew that this was the lifestyle she wanted for the future.

She imagined laughing with a man in the kitchen while she washed up, and feeling his arms wrap around her as she stood at the sink. She thought about romantic walks through the fields, hand-on-hand with her perfect man. She thought about waking up in the morning and knowing without turning over that the one person in the world who would love her forever, no matter what, was lying next to her.

And each time, the man in her daydreams was tall and unshaven and had a lock of hair that fell forwards over one eye.

The cat looked at her and she looked back.

'I know, I know, less dreaming and more stroking.'

She petted him for a few more minutes before she stopped, but as she did so she finally acknowledged to herself that she would never finish dreaming about Nick.

***

In the second week of the month, The Black Cat Gallery was featured in the home style pull-outs of a national newspaper, and Eleanor's trade tripled overnight. She had given the interview over the phone a week before Christmas and had sent in photos of the gallery as it had been when it was first opened. As the article had not appeared in the next few issues, she had forgotten all about it, thinking that they had decided against using it.

The visitors who came to Stourton loved the gallery, they loved Rosie's pottery and they loved the area. Many of them had come down for the weekend and were looking for recommendations of other attractions to visit and of places to stay overnight. Eleanor found that she was acting as a sort of unofficial Tourist Information Office for the area, and more than once saw people looking up at her windows as if wondering whether they had any vacancies.

By replacing a large table in the entrance hall with a smaller one, Eleanor was able to include a small rack for leaflets about local attractions, and found that word soon got round.

Soon after, the owner of a local Bed and Breakfast came to buy some of the honey she stocked and saw the rack.

'Ah ha! I'm always on the look-out for places to advertise. Would you mind if I dropped of a pile of my leaflets to put in your rack?'

Eleanor was happy to do this, 'As long as I can put some in the rack in your breakfast room,' she bargained.

'Of course,' the lady was more than happy to return the favour, 'And we should talk about websites, too. We should really get our websites linked together. Are you on the Stourton Village website?'

Eleanor was, and the two ladies agreed to speak to the other advertisers about forming a web ring so that prospective customers were guided from one site to the next.

The countryside around the gallery looked beautiful at this time of year. The grass verges were filled with poppies, vetch and the little white flowers known locally as shirt-buttons. The fields were a patchwork of amber, red, yellow, green and even blue where some farmers had started to grow linseed.

Once a week Eleanor drove into Stourton. The road from the gallery into town took her through a leafy green tunnel created by the trees which reached across the road towards each other, entwining their branches in a lovers embrace. The depth of the shadows underneath always took her by surprise and her car reacted by turning on the automatic headlights. Her journeys were erratic, slowed by joggers, bikes, tractors and hedge-cutters. At this time of year she never seemed to be able to go directly to her destination, but she had accepted this as a natural part of living in the country and loved to see the farmers shedding bits from their loads of hay as they took them back to be stored for winter use. Even the slow journey through the tunnel of trees seemed like an opportunity to marvel at the paintbrush splashed of light as they shimmered on the floor rather than a nuisance to be endured.

The only thorn in Eleanor's side was Nick Preston. She hardly saw him, but when she did he always looked so stern and determined that she only ever spoke to him briefly. Her breath still quickened when she saw him, and she caught herself involuntarily moving to be near him, but she knew that it was for the best that they stayed apart.

If only things had turned out differently. If only she and Nick had both been staying in the area they might have been able to start a relationship. On the rare occasions that they had worked together, they had seemed to complement each other perfectly, both understanding implicitly what it was that the other one needed and providing it without ceremony.

She thought briefly about going out to Australia, but laughed at herself and how foolish an idea that would be. After all, she hardly knew the man.

Even so, she couldn't help thinking how great her life would be with him in it. During the day they would run the gallery together and at night he would join her in the bed with the vintage quilt. She even started to think about what it would be like to have his children, imagining what a great father he would be.

How foolish, she thought and smiled sadly because it was only a dream.

***

Rosie was still staying with her and it was a comfort to have her friend with her in the evenings. They each had their own work to complete each day but in the evenings they made dinner together and chatted about their respective businesses.

'We're becoming like an old married couple,' joked Eleanor.

Rosie was still keen to run a Bed and Breakfast and each week she looked in the papers for a suitable property, poring over the tiny newsprint with a calculator on one side and her laptop on the other, searching for the perfect place. The large kitchen had become an impromptu office, and Eleanor had brought in an extra table so that each lady could have their own space.

'What a shame The Black Cat isn't large enough,' Rosie said, one evening, 'or I might be able to convince the owners to sell it to me.'

'They must be getting thousands for the plot now it comes with planning permission,' Eleanor reminded her. 'Much more than the price of the building on its own.'

'Still, it is in the most beautiful position, and you do have all these potential customers right on your doorstep.'

As they sat enjoying their coffee, Nick came and knocked on the back door. Seeing Rosie there, he hesitated. Rosie took the hint and said that she was going to her bedroom to work on some sketches for a new range of mugs she was designing.

'Um, Kate asked me to call round and speak to you personally,' he started.

Eleanor was confused. Apart from the disastrous two-minute meeting in the stables, she hadn't really spoken to Kate.

He saw the look on her face and stuttered, 'Kate - my sister - your landlady.'

Having Nick in her house again had put her brain in a spin, and she seemed to be seeing things through a thick fog, but Eleanor now began to see the truth.

'Kate *Wilkinson*?' she asked. '*Katherine* Wilkinson?'

'Yes,' he continued, 'She married an Australian while she was out there on her gap year. She asked me to come over and remind you that the lease ends on the 31st of July, but that she can extend it a month if you want because the developers are a bit behind.'

'Your sister owns this house?' after weeks of avoiding him, she now stood in front of him looking straight up into his liquid brown eyes. She could hardly think straight as he body leaned involuntarily in towards his.

'Yes, it was part of the old Stourton Hall estate. That's why it was called The Hall Arms when it was a pub. I thought you knew that.' He crossed his arms, then put his hands in his pockets, seemingly unsure of what to do with them.

'No,' said Eleanor, weakly, sitting down, 'but a lot of things are suddenly getting clearer. More clear,' she ground to a halt as her mouth seemed unable to keep up with her brain.

'So that's why you have a studio in the stables,' she was thinking out loud now, 'and why there's a path from my... your... this car park to your house.'

He nodded and started to back towards the door. 'Anyway, I've cleared out the studio and I've passed on the message about the lease, so you might not see me again,' he turned back to her, his eyes clouded with emotion, his mouth slightly open as if he was about to say something important. 'I'm sorry….I can't do this.' And he left.

Two days later she was woken to the sound of hammering as a For Sale sign was erected at the front gate. She rang the HR department at her old place of work and booked a meeting at which she could to speak to them about returning to her old job.

Chapter Twenty-Two

The summer days were long and hot, reminding Eleanor of the first summer she had been here. She had been to London to speak to HR and the noise and dust of the city had been a shock to her. All the time she was there she had longed to be back in the quiet of the Kentish countryside with the wide open space all around her.

This was, after all The Garden of England, and the fields were full of a variety of crops. Cherries were in season, and the vines in the hop fields were racing up the hop poles, the hop flowers just becoming visible through the thick foliage.

Eleanor loved to walk along the lanes, breathing in the fresh air and hearing the song of the skylark. She had bought herself a Birdsong DVD and had learnt the names and songs of all the local birds.

The gallery business was booming, and Eleanor was inundated with calls and visits from artists wanting to exhibit with her and to have their work in the Blue Moon Gallery. She worked with a local web designer to update her and was now offering prints for sale via the internet. Sales of these were up and she spent some of her time finding partner sites where she could further advertise the work.

Rosie had moved back into her own home. Daniel was coming home earlier than they had anticipated and she wanted to get everything ready for him. Her search for a suitable property that they could run as a Bed and Breakfast had so far failed and they were once more looking at extending their own property.

The shop was back up and running again and seemed to be doing well. Rosie had employed an assistant to run the shop so that she could spend time actually throwing the pots she sold. Luckily, her studio had escaped a lot of the flood damage and she had been able to salvage a lot of the materials.

Audrey was still a regular visitor to the gallery and had surprised everyone by finding husband number four living right on her doorstep.

She had come round to the gallery one day looking very smug and pleased with herself, and Eleanor had immediately asked her why.

Audrey sat at the kitchen table with her handbag on her knees and Eleanor could tell by the girlish expression on her face what her news was going to be.

'Don't tell me you've got a new cat,' she guessed, teasing her friend. 'Let me put the kettle on and you can tell me all about it.'

'Oh no, dear, that's not it at all,' Audrey corrected her, 'but I did want to ask you something.'

Eleanor left the tea things, and sat down at the table, worried by Audrey's serious tone. Perhaps her guess that a romance was on the cards had been wrong.

'I'm not sure if this is the sort of thing one can ask out of the blue,' she started, 'but I'd be most honoured if you would be one of the witnesses at my wedding.'

Eleanor laughed delightedly, 'Of course!' She gave Audrey a quick kiss and went back to making the tea, 'I've love to! Who's the lucky man?'

Audrey started a long rambling tale about one of her cats going missing and accidentally getting locked into the garden shed of one of her neighbours.

Eleanor listened, glad that somebody's love life was going well. The nice gentleman who owned the shed had helped Audrey to take the cat to the vet's surgery and had stayed with her while it was treated.

When the story came to its conclusion, Eleanor had to laugh again. It wasn't the nice old gentleman that Audrey was marrying – it was the vet!

'What about the chap with the shed?' Eleanor asked, when the story had finished.

'Oh, gosh,' said Audrey, shaking her head and shuddering slightly, 'I could never marry him. He reads the Daily Mail,'

Eleanor laughed again. The visit had done her good. When it was time for Audrey to leave, they embraced on the doorstep.

'You cheer me up every time you come round,' she told her friend, 'You must make sure you don't stop coming to see me after the wedding.'

'We're kindred spirits, aren't we?' replied Audrey as she walked across the gravel to her car. 'I think we'll always remain friends.'

The women waved to each other and then Audrey got into her car and drove away. Looking up into the sky, Eleanor noticed that the white cotton-wool clouds that she had noticed in the morning had been replaced by a blanket of grey. She shivered and quickly moved out of the shadows they cast, thinking about the speed with which things can change.

***

Eleanor read in the local paper that the Preston family were due to leave for Australia soon. The journalist made a big deal out of the fact that the Preston family had been in the area for generations and were now deserting the local townsfolk. Eleanor felt that she could second that thought.

Feeling that everybody had their lives sorted out except her, Eleanor drove out to the stone circle she had visited with Nick. The place had a sense of ancient permanence that gave her comfort.

She parked the car and found the path through the woods, hearing the cooing sound of the woodpigeons as she walked and breathing in the smell of the damp earth, protected from the summer sun by the solid canopy of leaves overhead.

Coming out into the light, she had to shield her eyes for a moment, adjusting to the brightness. She climbed up onto a fallen stone and stood as still as she could. She tried to imagine how many other people had stood here, as she was doing, looking out over the miles of countryside. She could see a tiny tractor working in a bright yellow field, leaving a caterpillar trail as it harvested the rape seed and she could hear the distant drone of a vehicle. It all seemed light years away.

Looking out onto the raw landscape below her, she wondered again about the people who had lived before her. She thought about their daily lives and came to the conclusion that they must have been fundamentally the same as her own. They would have loved and lost love, in exactly the same way that we do today. This comforted her, somehow, and she felt a deep connection with the past.

She thought about how much she had achieved in the past year. She was now a completely different person from the girl who had arrived in Stourton the year before, changed by the series of events that had befallen her and by her reactions to those events.

But most of all, she had been changed by her relationship with one man. She had not previously realised the depth of feeling that lay within her. She had lived her life until the point she had met him as if she had been in a daze; a fog had been lifted from around her on the day she had first looked into his eyes.

She saw now that it had been madness not to follow her heart. She had thrown away the one thing that mattered. All the jobs, all the money, all the property in the world were nothing compared to having the opportunity to live your life with the man you loved.

She closed her eyes, letting the sun warm her face and the breeze blow through her hair, hoping an answer would come to her; hoping that a miracle would occur and that somehow everything would be made all right. It was almost a prayer.

And as she did so, she heard a voice call her name. His voice. She thought at first that the voice was an echo in her mind, but as she opened her eyes and turned, she saw him standing there. Her beautiful man, lit by the golden glow of the evening sun.

She opened her arms and her heart to him as he moved towards her in one long stride and lifted her off the rocks, swinging her to the ground. He began to kiss her before her feet hit the ground and she felt as if they never would.

When he broke away and looked down into her eyes his face was serious.

'I couldn't go,' he said, simply, his eyes never leaving hers. 'I couldn't leave you.

She laughed, and kissed him again. 'I am *so* pleased, because I had just decided I might have to go to Australia to find you.'

His slow smile meant more to her than all the laughter or declarations that anyone else could have given.

***

One year on, Eleanor is still living at The Black Cat Gallery, although several things have changed in her life.

Rosie and Daniel have rented Stourton Hall Farm from Nick's parents and are now running it as successful Bed and Breakfast. Rosie had thought of the idea when she saw the newspaper article about the family moving. The building had looked so fabulous in the photograph that she had realised it would be the ideal property for her new business.

Taking the bull by the horns, she had driven straight over to the farm and rung the doorbell. Looking round at the mellowed red brick, mullioned windows and Kent peg roofs, she thought again how perfect it would be.

The door was opened by Nick's mother, Mrs Preston, who, although surprised to see Rosie, recognised her from her shop in town, and invited her in.

The women were of similar ages, and although from very different backgrounds, seemed to have a lot in common. The spent almost an hour chatting before Mrs Preston asked Rosie why she had called.

Rosie took a deep breath, 'I saw the For Sale board up outside and had a look at the details with the estate agent,' she started, 'Daniel and I would love to buy it, but we just don't have that sort of capital. I wondered if you'd be open to the idea of renting it to us?'

Rosie's open, good-natured face showed every emotion, and Mrs Preston could see how desperate she was to rent the house.

'Well, we did want to sell it outright so that we had the capital behind us when we went to Australia' she mused,' but I think we might be open to negotiations.' She was immediately enveloped in a huge bear hug from Rosie, who sat back quickly in her chair.

'Oh, sorry,' she blustered, evidently not very sorry at all. 'Would it be possible for me to have a look round? I am *so* pleased!'

Mrs Preston put a hand on her arm, 'We're just opening the talks, you know. This might not come to anything in the end,' she warned.

'Oh, I know,' said Rosie, 'It's just that I *really* want this house and I've got a feeling that it's all going to work out OK.' Her wild hair had untangled itself from her headband and was flying around her head. The look of pure joy on her face was infectious.

'Come on then,' said her potential landlady, 'Let me show you the estate.'

Eight weeks later the papers had been signed and Rosie and Daniel were the proud owners of a ten year lease for Stourton Hall Farm. The Prestons had been glad, in the end that the ownership of the property would stay in the family. The monthly rent would be more than enough for their needs in Australia, and the lease could be renegotiated at any time if either side wanted.

It didn't take long before a Bed and Breakfast sign went up outside. Starting with just four rooms, they were planning to build up the business slowly.

Nick and Eleanor bought The Black Cat Gallery from Kate at well below her asking price, and it has hardly changed since Eleanor lived there on her own. They make a fair living from the gallery, the art courses and Nick's furniture business.

Most importantly, Eleanor has changed her name. She is now Eleanor Preston, proud mother of six-week-old Evie.

Almost every morning she wakes to find Nick playing with the daughter he adores. During the day, Evie stays in the gallery with her mother, charming the visitors with the slow, sweet smile she inherited from her father. Nick runs his business from the workshop at Stourton Hall Farm or works in his studio.

In the evenings she is taken for long walks in the countryside. Already she is learning the songs of the birds and the voices of the trees as they sway with the wind between their leaves.

Looking out of her bedroom window, Eleanor sees them returning from one of their walks and waves. As she turns to run downstairs to meet them she sees Darwin looking at her from his favourite spot on the end of her bed. She stops to stroke him, and pauses for a moment.

'You see, Darwin, if you don't stop believing then dreams really can come true.'

www.ingramcontent.com/pod-product-compliance
Lightning Source LLC
Chambersburg PA
CBHW070924130626
46555CB00001B/272